Little Meg's Children by Hesba Stretton

Hesba Stretton was the pen name of Sarah Smith who was born on July 27th 1832 in Wellington, Shropshire, the younger daughter of bookseller, Benjamin Smith and his wife, Anne Bakewell Smith, a devout Methodist. Although she and her elder sister attended the Old Hall school in town, they were largely self-educated.

Smith became one of the most popular Evangelical writers of the 19th century. She used her "Christian principles as a protest against specific social evils in her children's books." Her moral tales and semi-religious stories, mainly directed towards the young, were printed in huge numbers.

After her sister submitted, without her knowledge, a story on her behalf ('The Lucky Leg', was a bizarre tale of a widower who proposes to women with wooden legs) Smith became a regular contributor to Household Words and All the Year Round, two popular periodicals begun by Charles Dickens. Dickens would collaborate with many writers to produce his part-work stories. Smith writing under the pseudonym Hesba Stretton (created from the initials of herself and four surviving siblings: **H**annah, **E**lizabeth, **S**arah, **B**enjamin, **A**nna and the name of a Shropshire village; All Stretton) contributed a well-regarded short story, 'The Ghost in the Cloak-Room', as part of 'The Haunted House'. She would go on to write over 40 novels.

Her break out book was 'Jessica's First Prayer', published in the Sunday at Home journal in 1866 and the following year as a book. By the end of the century it had sold over one and a half million copies. To put that into context; ten times the sales of 'Alice in Wonderland'. The book gave rise to a strand of books about homeless children in Victorian society combining elements of the sensational novel and the religious tract bringing the image of the poor, under-privileged, child into the Victorian social conscious.

A sequel, 'Jessica's Mother', was published in Sunday at Home in 1866 and eventually as a book, some decades later, in 1904. It was translated into fifteen European and Asiatic languages as well as Braille, depicted on coloured slides for magic lantern segments of Bands of Hope programmes, and placed in all Russian schools by order of Tsar Alexander II.

Smith became the chief writer for the Religious Tract Society. Her experience of working with slum children in Manchester in the 1860s gave her books great atmosphere and, of course, a sense of authenticity.

In 1884, Smith was one of the co-founders, together with Lord Shaftesbury and others, of the London Society for the Prevention of Cruelty to Children, which then combined, five years later, with societies in other cities to form the National Society for the Prevention of Cruelty to Children. Smith resigned a decade later in protest at financial mismanagement.

In retirement in Richmond, Surrey, the Smith sisters ran a branch of the Popular Book Club for working-class readers.

Sarah Smith died on October 8th, 1911 at home at Ivycroft on Ham Common. She had survived her sister by eight months.

Index of Contents

CHAPTER I

Motherless

In the East End of London, more than a mile from St Paul's Cathedral, and lying near to the docks, there is a tangled knot of narrow streets and lanes, crossing and running into one another, with blind alleys and courts leading out of them, and low arched passages, and dark gullies, and unsuspected slums, hiding away at the back of the narrowest streets; forming altogether such a labyrinth of roads and dwellings, that one needs a guide to thread a way among them, as upon pathless solitudes or deserts of shifting sands. In the wider streets it is possible for two conveyances to pass each other; for in some of them, towards the middle of their length, a sweeping curve is taken out of the causeway on either side to allow of this being done; but in the smaller and closer streets there is room spared only for the passage to and fro of single carts, while here and there may be found an alley so narrow that the neighbours can shake hands, if they would, from opposite windows. Many of the houses are of three or four stories, with walls, inside and out, dingy and grimed with smoke, and with windows that scarcely admit even the gloomy light which finds a way through the thick atmosphere, and down between the high, close buildings.

A few years ago in one of these dismal streets there stood a still more dismal yard, bearing the name of Angel Court, as if there yet lingered among those grimy homes and their squalid occupants some memories of a brighter place and of happier creatures. Angel Court was about nine feet wide, and contained ten or twelve houses on each side, with one dwelling at the further end, blocking up the thoroughfare, and commanding a view down the close, stone-paved yard, with its interlacing rows of clothes-lines stretched from window to window, upon which hung the yellow, half-washed rags of the inhabitants. This end house was three stories high, without counting a raised roof of red tiles, forming two attics; the number of rooms in all being eight, each one of which was held by a separate family, as were most of the other rooms in the court. To possess two apartments was almost an undreamed-of luxury.

There was certainly an advantage in living in the attics of the end house in Angel Court, for the air was a trifle purer there and the light clearer than in the stories below. From the small windows might be seen the prospect, not only of the narrow court, but of a vast extent of roofs, with a church spire here and there, and the glow of the sky behind them, when the sun was setting in a thick purplish cloud of smoke and fog. There was greater quiet also, and more privacy up in the attics than beneath, where all day long people were trampling up and down the stairs, and past the doors of their neighbours' rooms. The steep staircase ended in a steeper ladder leading up to the attics, and very few cared to climb up and down it. It was perhaps for these reasons that the wife of a sailor, who had gone to sea eight months before, had chosen to leave a room lower down, for which he had paid the rent in advance, in order to mount into higher and quieter quarters with her three children.

Whatever may have been her reason, it is certain that the sailor's wife, who had been ailing before her husband's departure, had, for some weeks past, been unable to descend the steep ladder into the maze of busy streets, to buy the articles necessary for her little household, and that she had steadily refused all aid from her neighbours, who soon left off pressing it upon her. The only nurse she had, and the only person to whom she would entrust her errands, was her eldest child, a small, spare, stunted girl of London growth, whose age could not be more than ten years, though she wore the shrewd, anxious air of a woman upon her face, with deep lines wrinkling her forehead and puckering about her keen eyes. Her small bony hands were hard with work; and when she trod to and fro about the crowded room, from the bedside to the fireplace, or from the crazy window to the creaking door, which let the cold draughts blow in upon the ailing mother, her step was slow and silent, less like that of a child than of a woman who was already weary with much labour. The room itself was not large enough to cause a great deal of work; but little Meg had had many nights of watching lately, and her eyes were heavy for want of sleep, with the dark circles underneath them growing darker every day.

The evening had drawn in, but Meg's mother, her head propped up with anything that could be made into a pillow, had watched the last glow of the light behind the chimneys and the church spires, and then she turned herself feebly towards the glimmer of a handful of coals burning in the grate, beside which her little daughter was undressing a baby twelve months old, and hushing it to sleep in her arms. Another child had been put to bed already, upon a rude mattress in a corner of the room, where she could not see him; but she watched Meg intently, with a strange light in her dim eyes. When the baby was asleep at last, and laid down on the mattress upon the floor, the girl went softly back to the fire, and stood for a minute or two looking thoughtfully at the red embers.

'Little Meg!' said her mother, in a low, yet shrill voice.

Meg stole across with a quiet step to the bedside, and fastened her eyes earnestly upon her mother's face.

'Do you know I'm going to die soon?' asked the mother.

'Yes,' said Meg, and said no more.

'Father'll be home soon,' continued her mother, 'and I want you to take care of the children till he comes. I've settled with Mr Grigg downstairs as nobody shall meddle with you till father comes back.

But, Meg, you've got to take care of that your own self. You've nothing to do with nobody, and let nobody have nothing to do with you. They're a bad crew downstairs, a very bad crew. Don't you ever let any one of 'em come across the door-step. Meg, could you keep a secret?'

'Yes, I could,' said Meg.

'I think you could,' answered her mother, 'and I'll tell you why you mustn't have nothing to do with the crew downstairs. Meg, pull the big box from under the bed.'

The box lay far back, where it was well hidden by the bed; but by dint of hard pulling Meg dragged it out, and the sailor's wife gave her the key from under her pillow. When the lid was open, the eyes of the dying woman rested with interest and longing upon the faded finery it contained—the bright-coloured shawl, and showy dress, and velvet bonnet, which she used to put on when she went to meet her husband on his return from sea. Meg lifted them out carefully one by one, and laid them on the bed, smoothing out the creases fondly. There were her own best clothes, too, and the children's; the baby's nankeen coat, and Robin's blue cap, which never saw the light except when father was at home. She had nearly emptied the box, when she came upon a small but heavy packet.

'That's the secret, Meg,' said her mother in a cautious whisper. 'That's forty gold sovereigns, as doesn't belong to me, nor father neither, but to one of his mates as left it with him for safety. I couldn't die easy if I thought it wouldn't be safe. They'd go rooting about everywhere; but, Meg, you must never, never, never let anybody come into the room till father's at home.'

'I never will, mother,' said little Meg.

'That's partly why I moved up here,' she continued. 'Why, they'd murder you all if they couldn't get the money without. Always keep the door locked, whether you're in or out; and, Meg dear, I've made you a little bag to wear round your neck, to keep the key of the box in, and all the money I've got left; it'll be enough till father comes. And if anybody meddles, and asks you when he's coming, be sure say you expect him home to-day or to-morrow. He'll be here in four weeks, on Robin's birthday, may be. Do you know all you've got to do, little Meg?'

'Yes,' she answered. 'I'm to take care of the children, and the money as belongs to one of father's mates; and I must wear the little bag round my neck, and always keep the door locked, and tell folks I expect father home to-day or to-morrow, and never let nobody come into our room.'

'That's right,' murmured the dying woman. 'Meg, I've settled all about my burial with the undertaker and Mr Grigg downstairs; and you'll have nothing to do but stay here till they take me away. If you like, you and Robin and baby may walk after me; but be sure see everybody out, and lock the door safe afore you start.'

She lay silent for some minutes, touching one after another the clothes spread upon the bed as Meg replaced them in the box, and then, locking it, put the key into the bag, and hung it round her neck.

'Little Meg,' said her mother, 'do you remember one Sunday evening us hearing a sermon preached in the streets?'

'Yes, mother,' answered Meg promptly.

'What was it he said so often?' she whispered. 'You learnt the verse once at school.'

'I know it still,' said Meg. '"If ye then, being evil, know how to give good gifts unto your children: how much more shall your Father which is in heaven give good things to them that ask Him?"'

'Ay, that's it,' she said faintly; 'and he said we needn't wait to be God's children, but we were to ask Him for good things at once, because He had sent His own Son to be our Saviour, and to die for us. "Them that ask Him, them that ask Him"; he said it over and over again. Eh! but I've asked Him a hundred times to let me live till father comes home, or to let me take baby along with me.'

'May be that isn't a good thing,' said Meg. 'God knows what are good things.'

The dying mother pondered over these words for some time, until a feeble smile played upon her wan face.

'It 'ud be a good thing anyhow,' she said, 'to ask Him to forgive me my sins, and take me to heaven when I die—wouldn't it, Meg?'

Yes, that's sure to be a good thing,' answered Meg thoughtfully.

'Then I'll ask Him for that all night,' said her mother, 'and to be sure take care of you all till father comes back. That 'ud be another good thing.'

She turned her face round to the wall with a deep sigh, and closed her eyelids, but her lips kept moving silently from time to time. Meg cried softly to herself in her chair before the fire, but presently she dozed a little for very heaviness of heart, and dreamed that her father's ship was come into dock, and she, and her mother, and the children were going down the dingy streets to meet him. She awoke with a start; and creeping gently to her mother's side, laid her warm little hand upon hers. It was deadly cold, with a chill such as little Meg had never before felt; and when her mother neither moved nor spoke in answer to her repeated cries, she knew that she was dead.

CHAPTER II

Little Meg as a Mourner

For the next day, and the night following, the corpse of the mother lay silent and motionless in the room where her three children were living. Meg cried bitterly at first; but there was Robin to be comforted, and the baby to be played with when it laughed and crowed in her face. Robin was nearly six years old, and had gained a vague, dim knowledge of death by having followed, with a troop of other curious children, many a funeral that had gone out from the dense and dirty dwellings to the distant cemetery, where he had crept forward to the edge of the grave, and peeped down into what seemed to him a very dark and dreadful depth. When little Meg told him mother was dead, and lifted him up to kneel on the bedside and kiss her icy lips for the last time, his childish heart was filled with an awe which almost made him shrink from the sight of that familiar face, scarcely whiter or more sunken now than it had been for many a day past. But the baby stroked the quiet cheeks, whilst chuckling and kicking in Meg's arms, and shouted, 'Mam! mam! mam!' until she caught it away, and pressing it tightly to her bosom, sat down on the floor by the bed, weeping.

'You've got no mam but me now, baby,' cried little Meg. She sat still for a while, with Robin lying on the ground beside her, his face hidden in her ragged frock; but the baby set up a pitiful little wail, and she put aside her own grief to soothe it.

'Hush! hush!' sang Meg, getting up, and walking with baby about the room. 'Hush, hush, my baby dear! By-by, my baby, by-by!'

Meg's sorrowful voice sank into a low, soft, sleepy tone, and presently the baby fell fast asleep, when she laid it upon Robin's little mattress, and covered it up gently with an old shawl. Robin was standing at the foot of the bed, gazing at his mother with wide-open, tearless eyes; and little Meg softly drew the sheet again over the pale and rigid face.

'Robbie,' she said, 'let's sit in the window a bit.'

They had to climb up to the narrow window-sill by a broken chair which stood under it; but when they were there, and Meg had her arm round Robin, to hold him safe, they could see down into Angel Court, and into the street beyond, with its swarms of busy and squalid people. Upon the stone pavement far below them a number of children of every age and size, but all ill-clothed and ill-fed, were crawling about, in and out of the houses, and their cries and shrieks came up to them in their lofty seat; but of late their mother had not let them run out to play in the streets, and they were mostly strangers to them except by sight. Now and then Meg and Robin cast a glance inwards at the quiet and still form of their mother, lying as if silently watching them with her half-closed eyes, and when they spoke to one another they spoke in whispers.

'Mother is going to live with the angels,' said Meg.

'What are angels?' asked Robin, his glittering black eyes glancing at the bed where she lay in her deep sleep.

'Oh, I'm not quite sure,' answered Meg. 'Only they're beautiful people, who are always white and clean, and shining, like that big white cloud up in the sky. They live somewhere up in the sky, where it's always sunny, and bright, and blue.'

'How 'll mother get up there?' inquired Robin.

'Well, I suppose,' replied Meg, after some reflection, 'after they've put her in the ground, the angels 'll come and take her away. I read once of a poor beggar, oh such a poor beggar! full of sores, and he died, and the angels carried him away somewhere. I thought, may be, they'd come for mother in the night; but I suppose they let people be buried first now, and fetch 'em away after.'

'I should like to see some angels,' said Robin.

They were silent again after that, looking down upon the quarrelling children, and the drunken men and women staggering about the yard below. Now and then a sharper scream rang through the court, as some angry mother darted out to cuff one or another of the brawling groups, or to yell some shrill reproach at the drunken men. No sound came to the ears of the listening children except the din and jarring tumult of the crowded city; but they could see the white clouds floating slowly across the sky over their heads, which seemed to little Meg like the wings of the waiting angels, hovering over the place where her mother lay dead.

'Meg,' said Robin, 'why do they call this Angel Court? Did the angels use to live here?'

'I don't think they ever could,' she answered sadly, 'or it must have been a long, long time ago. Perhaps they can't come here now, so they're waiting for mother to be taken out to the burying-ground afore they can carry her up to the sky. May be that's it.'

'Meg,' whispered Robin, pressing closer to her side, 'what's the devil?'

'Oh, I don't know,' cried Meg; 'only he's dreadfully, dreadfully wicked.'

'As wicked as father is when he's drunk?' asked Robin.

'Oh, a hundred million times wickeder,' answered Meg eagerly. 'Father doesn't get drunk often; and you mustn't be a naughty boy and talk about it.'

It was already a point of honour with little Meg to throw a cloak over her father's faults; and she spoke so earnestly that Robin was strongly impressed by it. He asked no more questions for some time.

'Meg,' he said at last, 'does the devil ever come here?'

'I don't think he does,' answered Meg, with a shrewd shake of her small head; 'I never see him, never. Folks are bad enough without him, I guess. No, no; you needn't be frightened of seeing him, Robbie.'

'I wish there wasn't any devil,' said Robin.

'I wish everybody in London was good,' said Meg.

They sat a while longer on the window-sill, watching the sparrows, all fluffy and black, fluttering and chattering upon the house-tops, and the night fog rising from the unseen river, and hiding the tall masts, which towered above the buildings. It was dark already in the court below; and here and there a candle had been lit and placed in a window, casting a faint twinkle of light upon the gloom. The baby stirred, and cried a little; and Meg lifted Robin down from his dangerous seat, and put two or three small bits of coal upon the fire, to boil up the kettle for their tea. She had done it often before, at the bidding of her mother; but it seemed different now. Mother's voice was silent, and Meg had to think of everything herself. Soon after tea was over she undressed Robin and the baby, who soon fell asleep again; and when all her work was over, and the fire put out, little Meg crept in beside them on the scanty mattress, with her face turned towards the bed, that she might see the angels if they came to carry her mother away. But before long her eyelids drooped over her drowsy eyes, and, with her arm stretched lightly across both her children, she slept soundly till daybreak.

No angels had come in the night; but early in the morning a neighbouring undertaker, with two other men, and Mr Grigg, the landlord, who lived on the ground-floor, carried away the light burden of the coffin which contained Meg's mother. She waited until all were gone, and then she locked the door carefully, and with baby in her arms, and Robin holding by her frock, she followed the funeral at a distance, and with difficulty, through the busy streets. The brief burial service was ended before they reached the cemetery, but Meg was in time to show Robin the plate upon the coffin before the grave-digger shovelled down great spadefuls of earth upon it. They stood watching, with sad but childish curiosity, till all was finished; and then Meg, with a heavy and troubled heart, took them home again to their lonely attic in Angel Court.

CHAPTER III

Little Meg's Cleaning Day

For a few days Meg kept up closely in her solitary attic, playing with Robin and tending baby; only leaving them for a few necessary minutes, to run to the nearest shop for bread or oatmeal. Two or three of the neighbours took the trouble to climb the ladder, and try the latch of the door, but they always found it locked; and if Meg answered at all, she did so only with the door between them, saying she was getting on very well, and she expected father home to-day or to-morrow. When she went in and out on her errands, Mr Grigg, a gruff, surly man, who kept everybody about him in terror, did not break his promise to her mother, that he would let no one meddle with her; and very quickly the brief interest of Angel Court in the three motherless children of the absent sailor died away into complete indifference, unmingled with curiosity: for everybody knew the full extent of their neighbours' possessions; and the poor furniture of Meg's room, where the box lay well hidden and unsuspected under the bedstead, excited no covetous desires. The tenant of the back attic, a girl whom Meg herself had seen no oftener than once or twice, was away on a visit of six weeks, having been committed to a House of Correction for being drunk and disorderly in the streets; so that by the close of the week in which the sailor's wife died no foot ascended or descended the ladder, except that of little Meg.

There were two things Meg set her heart upon doing before father came home: to teach Robin his letters, and baby to walk alone. Robin was a quick, bright boy, and was soon filled with the desire to surprise his father by his new accomplishment; and Meg and he laboured diligently together over the Testament, which had been given to her at a night school, where she had herself learned to read a little. But with the baby it was quite another thing. There were babies in the court, not to be compared with Meg's baby in other respects, who, though no older, could already crawl about the dirty pavement and down into the gutter, and who could even toddle unsteadily, upon their little bare feet, over the stone flags. Meg felt it as a sort of reproach upon her, as a nurse, to have her baby so backward. But the utmost she could prevail upon it to do was to hold hard and fast by a chair, or by Robin's fist, and gaze across the great gulf which separated her from Meg and the piece of bread and treacle stretched out temptingly towards her. It was a wan, sickly baby with an old face, closely resembling Meg's own, and meagre limbs, which looked as though they would never gain strength enough to bear the weight of the puny body; but from time to time a smile kindled suddenly upon the thin face, and shone out of the serious eyes—a smile so sweet, and unexpected, and fleeting, that Meg could only rush at her, and catch her in her arms, thinking there was not such another baby in the world. This was the general conclusion to Meg's efforts to teach her to walk, but none the less she put her through the same course of training a dozen times a day.

Sometimes, when her two children were asleep, little Meg climbed up to the window-sill and sat there alone, watching the stars come out in that sky where her mother was gone to live. There were nights when the fog was too thick for her to see either them or the many glittering specks made by the lamps in the maze of streets around her; and then she seemed to herself to be dwelling quite alone with Robin and baby, in some place cut off both from the sky above and the earth beneath. But by-and-by, as she taught Robin out of the Testament, and read in it herself two or three times a day, new thoughts of God and His life came to her mind, upon which she pondered, after her childish fashion, as she sat in the dark, looking out over the great vast city with its myriads of fellow-beings all about her, none of whom had any knowledge of her loneliness, or any sympathy with her difficulties.

After a week was past, Meg and her children made a daily expedition down to the docks, lingering about in any out-of-the-way corner till they could catch sight of some good-natured face, which threatened no unkind rebuff, and then Meg asked when her father's ship would come in. Very often she could get no satisfactory answer, but whenever she came across any one who knew the Ocean King, she heard that it would most likely be in dock by the end of October. Robin's birthday was the last day in October, so her mother's reckoning had been correct. Father would be home on Robbie's birthday; yet none the less was Meg's anxious face to be seen day after day about the docks, seeking someone to tell her over again the good news.

The last day but one arrived, and Meg set about the scrubbing and the cleaning of the room heartily, as she had seen her mother do before her father's return. Robin was set upon the highest chair, with baby on his lap, to look on at Meg's exertions, out of the way of the wet flooring, upon which she bestowed so much water that the occupant of the room below burst out upon the landing, with such a storm of threats and curses as made her light heart beat with terror. When the cleaning of the room was done, she trotted up and down the three flights of stairs with a small can, until she had filled, as full as it would hold, a broken tub, which was to serve as a bath for Robin and baby. It was late in the evening when all was accomplished, and Meg looked around her with a glow of triumph on the clean room and the fresh faces of the children. Very weary she felt, but she opened her Testament, in which she had not had time to give Robin a lesson that day, and she read a verse half aloud to herself.

'Come unto Me, all ye that labour and are heavy laden, and I will give you rest.'

'I wish I could go to Jesus,' sighed little Meg, 'for I've worked very hard all day; and He says He'd give me rest. Only I don't know where to go.'

She laid her head down on the pillow beside the baby's slumbering face, and almost before it rested there a deep sleep had come. Perhaps Meg's sigh had gone to Jesus, and it was He who gave her rest; 'for so He giveth His beloved sleep.'

CHAPTER IV

Little Meg's Treat to Her Children

Robin's birthday dawned brightly, even into the dark deep shadows of Angel Court, and Meg was awakened by the baby's two hands beating upon her still drowsy face, and trying to lift up her closed eyelids with its tiny fingers. She sprang up with a light heart, for father was coming home to-day. For the first time since her mother's death she dragged the box from under the bed, and with eager hands unlocked the lid. She knew that she dare not cross the court, she and the children, arrayed in the festive finery, without her father to take care of them; for she had seen other children stripped of all their new and showy clothes before they could reach the shelter of the larger streets.

But Meg was resolved that Robin and baby at least should not meet their father in rags. She took out the baby's coat and hood, too small now even for the little head it was to cover, and Robin's blue cap and brown holland pinafore. These things she made up into a bundle, looking longingly at her own red frock, and her bonnet with green ribbons: but Meg shook her head at herself admonishingly. It never would do to risk an appearance in such gorgeous attire. The very utmost she could venture upon was to put some half-worn shoes on her own feet and Robin's; for shoes were not in fashion for the children of Angel Court, and the unusual sound of their tread would attract quite as much attention as little Meg dare risk. She dressed her children and set them on the bed, while she put her own rough hair as smooth as she could by a little glass in the lid of the trunk. Her bonnet, which had originally belonged to her mother, had been once of black silk, but it was now brown with years, and the old shawl she pinned over the ragged bodice of her frock was very thin and torn at the edges; but Meg's heart was full of hope, and nothing could drive away the smile from her careworn face this morning. With the baby in her arms she carefully descended the ladder, having put the door-key into the bag round her neck along with the key of the box and her last half-crown. Then with stealthy steps she stole along under the houses, hushing Robin, who was inclined to make an unnecessary clatter in his shoes; but fortunately the inhabitants of Angel Court were not early risers, and Meg was off in good time, so they reached the outer streets safely, without notice or attack. Before going down to the docks Meg drew Robin into an empty archway, and there exchanged his ragged cap and pinafore for those she had put up into her bundle. Having dressed the baby also, she sat and looked at them both for a minute in mute admiration and delight. There could not be a prettier boy than Robin in all London, she was sure, with his bright black eyes and curly hair, that twisted so tightly round her fingers. As for the baby with her shrewd old-womanish face, and the sweet smile which spoke a good deal plainer than words, Meg could scarcely keep from kissing her all the time. How pleased and proud father would be! But when she remembered how she should have to tell him that mother was dead and buried, and none of them would ever see her again, Meg's eyes were blinded with tears, and hiding her face in the baby's neck, she cried, whether for joy or sorrow she could hardly tell; until Robin broke out into a loud wail of distress and terror, which echoed noisily under the low vault of the archway.

Little Meg roused herself at the sound of Robin's cry, and taking his hand in hers, with the baby upon her arm, she loitered about the entrance to the dockyard, till a good-tempered looking burly man came near to them. Meg planted herself bravely in his way, and looked up wistfully into his red face.

'Please, sir,' she said, 'could you tell me if father's ship's come in yet?'

'Father's ship!' repeated the man in a kindly voice. 'Why, what's the name of father's ship?'

'The Ocean King,' said Meg, trembling.

'It's in the river, my little lass,' he said, 'but it won't be in dock till night. Father can't be at home afore to-morrow morning at the soonest.'

'Thank you kindly, sir,' answered Meg, her voice faltering with her great joy. Her task was ended, then. To-morrow she would give up the key of the box with its secret treasure, which she hardly dared to think about, and then she could feel like a child once more. She did feel almost as gay as Robin who was pattering and stamping proudly along in his shoes, and in the consciousness that it was his birthday.

Nobody else had such a thing as a birthday, so far as he knew; certainly none of his acquaintances in Angel Court, not even Meg herself, for Meg's birthday was lost in the depth of the ten years which had passed over her head. He scarcely knew what it was, for he could neither see it nor touch it; but he had it, for Meg told him so, and it made him feel glad and proud. It was a bright, warm, sunny autumn day, with enough freshness in the breeze coming off the unseen river to make the air sweet and reviving; for Meg was skirting about the more open streets, without venturing to pass through the closer and dirtier alleys.

'Robbie,' she said after a time, when they had come to a halt upon the steps of a dwelling-house, 'Robbie, I'll give you a treat to-day, because it's your birthday. We'll not go home till it's dark; and I'll take you to see Temple Gardens.'

'What are Temple Gardens?' demanded Robin, his eyes eager for an answer.

'Oh, you'll see,' said Meg, not quite able to explain herself. 'I went there once, ever so many years ago, when I was a little girl. You'll like 'em ever so!'

'Do we know the road?' asked Robin doubtfully.

'I should think so!' replied Meg; 'and if we didn't, there's the police. What's the police good for, if they couldn't tell a person like me the road to Temple Gardens? We'll have such a nice day!'

The children trotted along briskly till they reached the broad thoroughfares and handsome shops of the main streets which traverse London, where a constant rush of foot passengers upon the pavement, and of conveyances in the roadway, hurry to and fro from morning to midnight. Poor little Meg stood for a few minutes aghast and stunned, almost fearful of committing herself and her children to the mighty stream; but Robin pulled her on impatiently. He had been once as far as the Mansion House, before the time when their mother's long illness had made them almost prisoners in their lonely attic; and Meg herself had wandered several times as far as the great church of St Paul. After the first dread was over, she found a trembling, anxious enjoyment in the sight of the shops, and of the well-dressed people in the streets. At one of the windows she was arrested by a full-size vision of herself, and Robin, and the baby, reflected in a great glass, a hundred times larger than the little square in the box-lid at home. She could not quite keep down a sigh after her own red frock and best bonnet; but she comforted herself quickly with the thought that people would look upon her as the nurse of Robin and baby, sent out to take them a walk.

They did not make very rapid progress, for they stopped to look in at many shop windows, especially where there were baby-clothes for sale, or where there were waxen figures of little boys, life-size, dressed in the newest fashions, with large eyes of glass beads, not unlike Robin's own black ones. The passage of the crossings was also long and perilous. Meg ran first with the baby, and put her down safely on the other side in some corner of a doorway; then with a sinking and troubled heart, least any evil person should pick her up, and run away with her as a priceless treasure, she returned for Robin. In this way she got over several crossings, until they reached the bottom of Ludgate Hill, where she stood shivering and doubting for a long time, till she fairly made up her mind to speak to the majestic policeman looking on calmly at the tumult about him.

'Oh, if you please, Mr Police,' said Meg, in a plaintive voice, 'I want to get these two little children over to the other side, and I don't know how to do it, except you'd please to hold baby while I take Robbie across.'

The policeman looked down from his great height, without bending his stiff neck, upon the childish creature who spoke to him, and Meg's spirit sank with the fear of being ordered back again. But he picked up Robin under his arm, and bidding her keep close beside him, he threaded his way through the throng of carriages. This was the last danger; and now with restored gaiety Meg travelled on with her two children.

[Illustration: The policeman picked up Robin under his arm, and threaded his way through the throng of carriages.]

By-and-by they turned from the busy Fleet Street under a low archway, and in a minute they were out of the thunder of the streets which had almost drowned their voices, and found themselves in a place so quiet and so calm, with a sort of grave hush in the very air, that Robin pressed close to Meg's side, with something of the silent and subdued awe with which he might have entered a church. There were houses here, and courts, but not houses and courts like those from which they had come. Here and there they came upon a long corridor, where the sun shone between the shadows of the pillars supporting the roof; and they looked along them with wondering eyes, not knowing where they could lead to, and too timid to try to find out. It was not a deserted place, but the number of people passing to and fro were few enough to make it seem almost a solitude to these poor children, who had travelled hither from the over-crowded slums of the East End. They could hear their own voices, when they spoke, ring out in such clear, echoing tones, that Meg hushed Robin, lest some of the grave, stern, thoughtful gentlemen who passed them should bid them begone, and leave the Temple to its usual stillness. The houses seemed to them so large and grand, that Meg, who had heard once of the Queen, and had a dim notion of her as a lady of extraordinary greatness and grandeur, whispered to Robin confidentially that she thought the Queen must live here.

They came upon a fountain in the centre of a small plot of grass and flowers, enclosed within high railings; and Robin uttered a shrill cry of delight, which rang noisily through the quiet court where its waters played in the sunshine. But at last they discovered, with hearts as eagerly throbbing as those of the explorers of some new country, the gardens, the real Temple Gardens! The chrysanthemums were in full blossom, with all their varied tints, delicate and rich, glowing under the brightness of the noontide sun; and Robin and Meg stood still, transfixed and silent, too full of an excess of happiness to speak.

'Oh, Meg, what is it? what is it?' cried Robin at last, with outstretched hands, as if he would fain gather them all into his arms. 'Is it gardens, Meg? Is this Temple Gardens?'

Meg could not answer at first, but she held Robin back from the flowers. She did not feel quite at home in this strange, sweet, sunny place; and she peeped in cautiously through the half-open iron gate before entering. There were a few other children there, with their nursemaids, but she felt there was some untold difference between her and them. But Robin's delight had given him courage, and he rushed in tumultuously, running along the smooth walks in an ecstasy of joy; and Meg could do nothing else but follow. Presently, as nobody took any notice of her, she gave herself up to the gladness of the hour, and toiled up and down, under the weight of the baby, wherever Robin wished to go, until he consented to rest a little while upon a seat which faced the river, where they could see the boats pass by. This was the happiest moment to Meg. She thought of her father's ship coming up the river, bringing him home to her and the children; and she had almost lost the recollection of where she was, when Robin, who had been very quiet for some time, pulled her by the shawl.

'Look, Meg,' he whispered.

He pointed to a seat not far from them, where sat a lady, in a bright silk dress, and a velvet bonnet with a long rich feather across it. There were two children with her, a girl of Meg's age, and a boy about as big as Robin, dressed like a little Highlander, with a kilt of many colours, and a silver-mounted pouch, and a dirk, which he was brandishing about before his mother, who looked on, laughing fondly and proudly at her boy. Meg gazed, too, until she heard Robin sob, and turning quickly to him, she saw the tears rolling quickly down his sorrowful face. 'Nobody laughs to me, Meg,' said Robin.

'Oh yes, Robbie, I laugh to you,' cried Meg; 'and father 'll laugh when he comes home to-morrow; and maybe God laughs to us, only we can't see His face.'

'I'd like to go home,' sobbed Robin; and Meg took her baby upon her tired arm, and turned her steps eastward once more. As they left Temple Gardens, languid and weary, Meg saw the friendly man who had spoken kindly to them that morning at the docks passing by in an empty dray, and meeting her wistful eyes, he pulled up for a minute.

'Hullo, little woman!' he shouted. 'Are you going my way?'

He pointed his whip towards St Paul's, and Meg nodded, for her voice could not have reached him through the din.

'Hoist them children up here, that's a good fellow,' he said to a man who was standing by idle; and in a few seconds more they were riding triumphantly along Fleet Street in such a thrill and flutter of delight as Meg's heart had never felt before, while Robin forgot his sorrows, and cheered on the horses with all the power of his shrill voice. The dray put them down at about half a mile from Angel Court, while it was still broad daylight, and Robin was no longer tired. Meg changed her last half-crown, and spent sixpence of it lavishly in the purchase of some meat pies, upon which they feasted sumptuously, in the shelter of a doorway leading to the back of a house.

CHAPTER V

Little Meg's Neighbour

When their feast was over, the children sauntered on slowly, not wishing to enter Angel Court till it was dark enough for Robin's and baby's finery to pass by unseen; but as soon as it was dark they turned out of the main thoroughfare into the dingy streets more familiar to them. As they entered the house Meg heard the deep gruff voice of Mr Grigg calling to her, and she went into his room, trembling, and holding the baby very tightly in her arms. It was a small room, the same size as their own attic, and the litter and confusion throughout made it impossible to go in more than a step or two. Mr Grigg was seated at a stained wooden table, upon which stood two large cups and a black bottle of gin, with a letter lying near to Mr Grigg's large and shaking hand. Coming in from the fresh air of the night, Meg coughed a little with the mingled fumes of gin and tobacco; but she coughed softly for fear of giving offence.

'Here's a letter come for your mother, little Meg,' said Mr Grigg, seizing it eagerly, 'I'll read it to you if you like.'

'Oh no, thank you, sir,' answered Meg quickly; 'father's coming home, and he'll read it to-morrow morning. His ship's in the river, and it'll be in dock to-night for certain. So he'll be home to-morrow.'

Upon hearing this news Mr Grigg thought it best to deliver up the letter to Meg, but he did it so reluctantly that she hurried away lest he should reclaim it. Robin was already halfway upstairs, but she soon overtook him, and a minute afterwards reached their own door. She was about to put the baby down to take out the key, when, almost without believing her own eyes, she saw that it was in the lock, and that a gleam of firelight shone through the chinks of the door. Meg lifted the latch with a beating heart, and looked in before venturing to enter. The fire was lighted, but there seemed to be no other disturbance or change in the attic since the morning, except that in her mother's low chair upon the hearth there sat a thin slight woman, like her mother, with the head bowed down, and the face hidden in the hands. Meg paused, wonder-stricken and speechless, on the door-sill; but Robin ran forward quickly, with a glad shout of 'Mother! mother!'

At the sound of Robin's step and cry the woman lifted up her face. It was a white, thin face, but younger than their mother's, though the eyes were red and sunken, as if with many tears, and there was a gloom upon it, as if it had never smiled a happy smile. Meg knew it in an instant as the face of the tenant of the back attic, who had been in jail for six weeks, and her eye searched anxiously the dark corner under the bed, where the box was hidden. It seemed quite safe and untouched, but still Meg's voice was troubled as she spoke.

'I thought I'd locked up all right,' she said, stepping into the room, while Robin took refuge behind her, and regarded the stranger closely from his place of safety.

'Ay, it was all right,' answered the girl, 'only you see my key 'd unlock it; and I felt cold and low coming out of jail to-day; and I'd no coal, nor bread, nor nothing. So I came in here, and made myself comfortable. Don't you be crusty, little Meg. You'd be the same if you'd been locked up for six weeks. I wish I were dead, I do.'

The girl spoke sadly, and dropped her head again upon her hands, while Meg stood in the middle of the floor, not knowing what to do or say. She sat down after a while upon the bedstead, and began taking off the baby's things, pondering deeply all the time what course of action she ought to follow. She could place herself so as to conceal completely the box under the bed; but if the girl's key would unlock her attic door, how was she ever to leave it for a moment in safety? Then the thought flashed across her that father would be at home to-morrow, and she would no longer have to take care of the hidden treasure. In the meantime Robin had stolen up to the stranger's side, and after closely considering her for some moments, he stroked her hand with his own small fingers.

'I thought you were mother, I did,' he said. 'It's my birthday to-day.'

For one instant the girl looked at him with a smile in her sunken eyes, and then she lifted him on to her lap, and laid her face upon his curly head, sobbing bitterly.

'Little Meg,' she said, 'your mother spoke kind to me once, and now she's dead and gone. I wonder why I wasn't took instead o' her?'

Meg's tender heart closed itself no longer against the stranger. She got up from her seat, and crossing the floor to the fireside, she put the baby down by Robin on her lap.

'You didn't ought to go into a person's room without asking leave,' she said; 'but if you'll hold baby for me, I'll soon get tea. I've got a little real tea left, and father 'll buy some more to-morrow. You mind the children till it's ready.'

It was soon ready, and they drank and ate together, with few words. Meg was intent upon getting her weary children to bed as soon as possible, and after it was over she undressed them at once. Before Robin got into bed she addressed the girl hesitatingly.

'Robbie always says his prayers aloud to me,' she said; 'you won't mind, will you?'

'Go on,' answered the girl, with a sob.

'Robbie,' said Meg, as he knelt at her knee, with his hands held up between both her hands, 'Robbie, it's your birthday to-day; and if I was you I'd ask God for something more than other days. I'd ask Him to bless everybody as well as us if I was you. If everybody was good, it'd be so nice.'

'Yes, Meg,' replied Robin promptly, closing his black eyes before he began his prayer. 'Pray God, bless father on the big sea, and bless me, and Meg, and baby, and take care of us all. Pray God, bless everybody, 'cept the devil. Amen.'

But Robin did not get up from his knees. He dropped his head upon Meg's lap, and when she moved he cried, 'Stop a minute!' Meg waited patiently until he lifted up his face again, and shutting his eyes very tightly, said, 'Pray God, bless everybody, and the devil, and make him a good man. Amen.'

'Robbie,' said Meg mournfully, 'I don't think the devil can be made good. He doesn't want to be good. If anybody wants to be good, God can make 'em good, anybody in all the world; but He won't if they don't want to.'

Robin was already half asleep, and gave little heed to Meg's words. She tucked him snugly into his place beside baby, and stooping over them, kissed both their drowsy faces with a loving and lingering tenderness. Then she turned to the fire, and saw the strange girl there upon her knees before her mother's chair, weeping again in a passion of tears.

CHAPTER VI

Little Meg's Last Money

'What's the matter with you?' asked Meg, laying her small rough hand upon the girl's head.

'Oh, Meg, Meg!' she cried, 'I do want to be good, and I can't. You don't know how wicked I am; but once I was a good little girl like you. And now I can never, never be good again.'

'Yes, you can,' answered little Meg, 'if you ask God.'

'You don't know anything about it,' she said, pushing away Meg's hand.

'I don't know much,' replied Meg meekly; 'but Jesus says in the Bible, that if our fathers 'll give us good things, God 'll much more give good things to anybody as asks for 'em.'

'But I'm too bad to ask Him,' said the girl.

'I don't know what's to be done, then,' answered Meg. 'The Bible says, "Those that ask Him"; and if you are too bad to ask Him, I suppose He won't give you any good things.'

The girl made no reply, but crouching down upon the hearth at Meg's feet, she sat looking into the fire with the expression of one who is thinking deeply. Meg too was silent for a time, smiling now and then as she recollected that father would be at home to-morrow.

'I don't know what you're called,' said Meg, after a very long silence.

'Oh, they call me Kitty, and Puss, and Madcap, and all sorts o' names,' answered the girl, with a deep sigh.

'But that's not your christen name?' said Meg.

'No,' she replied.

'What does your mother call you?' asked Meg.

For a moment little Meg was terrified, for the girl seized her hands in a strong and painful grasp, and her red eyes flamed with anger; but she loosed her hold gradually, and then, in a choking voice, she said, 'Don't you never speak to me about my mother!'

'Have you got any money, Kitty?' inquired Meg, by way of turning the conversation.

'Not a rap,' said Kitty, laughing hoarsely.

'I've got two shillings left,' continued Meg, 'and I'll give you one; only, if you please, you mustn't come into my room again, at least till father's at home. I promised mother not to let anybody at all come here. You'll not be angry, will you?'

'No, I'm not angry,' said Kitty gently, 'and you must always do what your mother told you, little Meg. She spoke kind to me once, she did. So I'll go away now, dear, and never come in again: but you wouldn't mind me listening at the door when Robbie's saying his prayers sometimes?'

'No,' answered Meg; 'and you may listen when I read up loud, if you like. I always read something afore I go to bed, and I'll speak up loud enough for you to hear.'

'I'll listen,' said Kitty, standing up to go to her own dark, cold attic, and looking round sadly at Meg's tidy room, all ready as it was for her father's arrival. 'I suppose you'd not mind me kissing the children afore I go?'

'Oh no,' said Meg, going with her to the bedside, and looking down fondly upon the children's sleeping faces. The baby's pale small face wore a smile upon it, as did Robin's also, for he was dreaming of the gardens he had visited on his birthday. The girl bent over them, but she drew back without kissing them, and with a sharp painful tone in her voice she said, 'I wish I was dead, I do.'

CHAPTER VII

Little Meg's Disappointment

If Meg had been up early on Robin's birthday, she was out of bed and about her preparations still earlier the next morning. She had time to go over again most of her brushing and rubbing of the scanty furniture before the children awoke. She reached out all their best clothes, and her own as well, for she did not intend to go down to the docks to meet her father, but thought it would be best to wait at home for his arrival. Her hands were full, and her thoughts also, for some time; and it was not till the nearest clock struck eleven that she could consider all her preparations completed.

When all her work was done, Meg helped Robin up to the window-sill, and climbed after him herself to the perilous seat, with the baby held fast upon her lap. It was the first time the baby had been allowed to occupy this dangerous place, and for the first few minutes Meg was not without her fears; but it was weary and languid this morning, and sat quite still upon her lap, with its little head resting upon her shoulder, and its grave eyes looking out inquiringly upon the strange world in which it found itself. Meg and Robin watched every man who entered the court; and every now and then Robin would clap his hands, and shout loudly, 'Father, father!' making Meg's arms tremble, and her heart beat fast with expectation. But it was nine months since he had gone away, and Robin had almost forgotten him, so that it always proved not to be her father. Hour after hour passed by, and Meg cut up the last piece of bread for the children and herself, and yet he never came; though they stayed faithfully at their post, and would not give up looking for him as long as the daylight lasted. But the night drew near at last, an early night, for it was the first day in November, and London fogs grow thick then; and Meg kindled the fire again, and sat down by it, unwilling to undress the children before he came. So she sat watching and waiting, until the baby fell into a broken, sobbing slumber on her lap, and Robin lay upon the floor fast asleep.

At length Meg resolved to lay the children in bed, dressed as they were, and steal down herself to the docks, under the shelter of the fog, to see if she could learn any news of the Ocean King. She drew the old shawl over her head, which well covered her red frock, and taking off her shoes and stockings—for father would not miss them in the night—she crept unseen and unheard down the dark staircase, and across the swarming, noisy court. The fog was growing thicker every minute, yet she was at no loss to find her way, so familiar it was to her. But when she reached the docks, the darkness of the night, as well as that of the fog, hid from her the presence of her good-natured friend, if indeed he was there. There were strange noises and rough voices to be heard, and from time to time the huge figure of some tall man appeared to her for an instant in the gloom, and vanished again before little Meg could find courage to speak to him. She drew back into a corner, and peered eagerly, with wistful eyes, into the thick yellow mist which hid everything from them, while she listened to the clank of iron cables, and the loud sing-song of the invisible sailors as they righted their vessels. If she could only hear her father's voice among them! She felt sure she should know it among a hundred others, and she was ready to cry aloud the moment it reached her ears—to call 'Father!' and he would be with her in an instant, and she in his arms, with her own clasped fast about his neck. Oh, if he would but speak out of the darkness! Meg's keen eyes grew dim with tears, and her ears seemed to become dull of hearing, from the very longing to see and hear more clearly. But she rubbed away the tears with her shawl, and pushed the tangled hair away behind her small ears, and with her hands pressed against her heart, to deaden its throbbing, she leaned forward to pierce, if possible, through the thick dark veil which separated her from her father.

She had been there a long time when the thought crossed her, that perhaps after all he had been knocking at the door at home, and trying to open it; waking up the children, and making them cry and scream with terror at finding themselves quite alone. She started up to hurry away; but at that moment a man came close by, and in the extremity of her anxiety Meg stopped him.

'Please,' she said earnestly, 'is the Ocean King come in yet?'

'Ay,' was the answer. 'Came in last night, all right and tight.'

'Father must be come home, then,' thought Meg, speeding away swiftly and noiselessly with her bare feet along the streets to Angel Court. She glanced up anxiously to her attic window, which was all in darkness, while the lower windows glimmered with a faint light from within. The landlord's room was full of a clamorous, quarrelling crew of drunkards; and Meg's spirit sank as she thought—suppose father had been up to their attic, and finding it impossible to get in at once, had come down, and begun to drink with them! She climbed the stairs quickly, but all was quiet there; and she descended again to hang about the door, and listen, and wait; either to discover if he was there, or to prevent him turning in when he did come. Little Meg's heart was full of a woman's heaviest care and anxiety, as she kept watch in the damp and the gloom of the November night, till even the noisy party within broke up, and went their way, leaving Angel Court to a brief season of quietness.

Meg slept late in the morning, but she was not disturbed by any knock at the door. Robin had crept out of bed and climbed up alone to the window-sill, where fortunately the window was shut and fastened; and the first thing Meg's eyes opened upon was Robin sitting there, in the tumbled clothes in which he had slept all night. The morning passed slowly away in mingled hope and fear; but no step came up the ladder to their door, and Kitty had gone out early in the morning, before Meg was awake. She spent her last shilling in buying some coal and oatmeal; and then, because it was raining heavily, she stationed herself on the topmost step of the stairs, with Robin and baby, waiting with ever-growing dread for the long-delayed coming of her father.

It was growing dark again before any footstep came further than the landing below, and then it was a soft, stealthy, slipshod step, not like the strong and measured tread of a man. It was a woman who climbed the steep ladder, and Meg knew it could be no one else but Kitty. The girl sat down on the top step beside them, and took Robin upon her lap.

'What are you all doing out here, little Meg?' she said, in a low, gentle voice, which Meg could scarcely believe to be the same as that which had sometimes frightened her by its shrill shrieks of drunken merriment.

'We're looking for father,' she answered weariedly. 'He's never come yet, and I've spent all my money, and we've got no candles.'

'Meg,' said Kitty, 'I can pay you back the shilling you gave me on Tuesday night.'

'But you mustn't come into our room, if you do,' answered Meg.

'No, no, I'll not come in,' said she, pressing a shilling into Meg's hand. 'But why hasn't father come home?'

'I don't know,' sobbed Meg. 'His ship came in the night of Robbie's birthday, that's two days ago; and he's never come yet.'

'The ship come in!' repeated Kitty, in a tone of surprise. 'What's the name o' the ship, Meg?'

'Father's ship's the Ocean King,' said Robin proudly.

'I'll hunt him up,' cried Kitty, rising in haste. 'I'll find him, if he's anywhere in London. I know their ways, and where they go to, when they come ashore, little Meg. Oh! I'll hunt him out. You put the children to bed, dear; and then you sit up till I come back, if it's past twelve o'clock, I'll bring him home, alive or dead. Don't cry no more, little Meg.'

She called softly up the stairs to say these last words, for she had started off immediately. Meg did as she had told her, and then waited with renewed hope for her return. It was past midnight before Kitty tapped quietly at the door, and she went out to her on the landing. But Kitty was alone, and Meg could hardly stand for the trembling which came upon her.

'Haven't you found father?' she asked.

'I've found out where he is,' answered Kitty. 'He's at the other end of the world, in hospital. He was took bad a-coming home—so bad, they was forced to leave him behind them; and he'll work his way back when he's well enough, so Jack says, one of his mates. He says he may come back soon, or come back late, and that's all he knows about him. What shall you do, little Meg?'

'Mother said I was to be sure to take care of the children till father comes home,' she answered, steadying her voice; 'and I'll do it, please God. I can ask Him to help me, and He will. He'll take care of us.'

'He hasn't took care o' me,' said Kitty bitterly.

'May be you haven't asked Him,' said Meg.

Kitty was silent for a minute, and then she spoke in a voice half choked with sobs.

'It's too late now,' she said, 'but He'll take care of you, never fear; and oh! I wish He'd let me help Him. I wish I could do something for you, little Meg; for your mother spoke kind to me once, and made me think of my own mother. There, just leave me alone, will you? I'm off to bed now, and you go to bed too. I'll help you all I can.'

She pushed Meg back gently into her attic, and closed the door upon her; but Meg heard her crying and moaning aloud in her own room, until she herself fell asleep.

CHAPTER VIII

Little Meg's Red Frock in Pawn

Meg felt very forlorn when she opened her heavy eyelids the next morning. It was certain now that her father could not be home for some time, it might be a long time; and how was she to buy bread for her children and herself? She took down her mother's letter from the end of a shelf which supplied the place of a chimney-piece, and looked at it anxiously; but she dared not ask anybody to read it for her, lest it should contain some mention of the money hidden in the box; and that must be taken care of in every way, because it did not belong to her, or father even, but to one of his mates. She had no friend to go to in all the great city. Once she might have gone to the teacher at the school where she had learned to read a little; but that had been in quite a different part of London, on the other side of the river, and they had moved from it before her father had started on his last voyage. Meg sat thinking and pondering sadly enough, until suddenly, how she did not know, her fears were all taken away, and her childish heart lightened. She called Robin, and bade him kneel down beside her, and folding baby's hands together, she closed her own eyes, and bowed her head, while she asked God for the help He had promised to give.

'Pray God,' said little Meg, 'You've let mother die, and father be took bad at the other side of the world, and there's nobody to take care of us 'cept You, and Jesus says, if we ask You, You'll give us bread and everything we want, just like father and mother. Pray God, do! I'm not a grown-up person yet, and Robin's a very little boy, and baby can't talk or walk at all; but there's nobody else to do anythink for us, and we'll try as hard as we can to be good. Pray God, bless father at the other side of the world, and Robbie, and baby, and me; and bless everybody, for Jesus Christ's sake. Amen.'

Meg rose from her knees joyfully, feeling sure that her prayer was heard and would be answered. She went out with her children to lay out the shilling Kitty had returned to her the day before; and when they come in she and Robin sat down to a lesson in reading. The baby was making a pilgrimage of the room from chair to chair, and along the bedstead; but all of a sudden she balanced herself steadily upon her tiny feet, and with a scream of mingled dread and delight, which made Meg and Robin look up quickly, she tottered across the open floor to the place where they were sitting, and hid her face in Meg's lap, quivering with joy and wonder. Meg's gladness was full, except that there was a little feeling of sorrow that neither father nor mother was there to see it.

'Did God see baby walk?' inquired Robin.

'I should think He did!' said Meg confidently; and her slight sorrow fled away. God could not help loving baby, she felt sure of that, nor Robin; and if He loved them, would He not take care of them Himself, and show her how to take care of them, till father was at home? The day passed almost as happily as Robin's birthday; though the rain came down in torrents, and pattered through the roof, falling splash, splash into the broken tub, with a sound something like the fountain in Temple Gardens.

But when Kitty's shilling was gone to the last farthing, and not a spoonful of meal remained in the bag, it was not easy to be happy. Robin and baby were both crying for food; and there was no coal to make a fire, nor any candle to give them light during the long dark evenings of November. Kitty was out all day now, and did not get home till late, so Meg had not seen her since the night she had brought the news about her father. But a bright thought came to her, and she wondered at herself for not having thought of it before. She must pawn her best clothes; her red frock and bonnet with green ribbons. There was a natural pang at parting with them, even for a time; but she comforted herself with the idea that father would get them back for her as soon as he returned. She reached them out of the box, feeling carefully lest she should take any of Robin's or the baby's by mistake in the dark; and then she set off with her valuable bundle, wondering how many shillings she would get for them, and whether she could make the money last till her father came. The pawnbroker's shop was a small, dingy place in Rosemary Lane; and it, and the rooms above it, were as full as they could be with bundles such as poor Meg carried under her old shawl. A single gas-light was flaring away in the window, and a hard-featured, sharp-eyed man was reading a newspaper behind the counter. Meg laid down her bundle timidly, and waited till he had finished reading his paragraph; after which he opened it, spread out the half-worn frock, and held up the bonnet on his fist, regarding them both with a critical and contemptuous eye. Some one else had entered the shop, but Meg was too absorbed and too anxious to take any heed of it. The pawnbroker rolled the frock up scornfully, and gave it a push towards her.

'Tenpence for the two,' he said, looking back at his newspaper.

'Oh! if you please,' cried little Meg, in an agony of distress, 'you must give me more than tenpence. I've got two little children, and no bread, nor coals, nor candles. I couldn't buy scarcely anythink with only tenpence. Indeed, indeed, my red frock's worth a great deal more; it's worth I don't know how many shillings.'

'You go home, little Meg,' said Kitty's voice behind her, 'and I'll bring you three shillings for the frock, and one for the bonnet; four for the two. Mr Sloman's an old friend o' mine, he is; and he'll oblige you for my sake. There, you run away, and I'll manage this little bit o' business for you.'

Meg ran away as she was told, glad enough to leave her business with Kitty. By-and-by she heard her coming upstairs, and went out to meet her. Kitty placed four shillings in her hand.

'Meg,' she said, 'you let me do that sort o' work for you always. They'll cheat you ever so; but I wouldn't, not to save my life, if you'll only trust me. You ask me another time. Is that the way God takes care of you?'

'He does take care of me,' answered Meg, with a smile; 'or may be you wouldn't have come into the shop just now, and I should have got only tenpence. I suppose that's taking care of me, isn't it?'

'I don't know,' said Kitty. 'Only let me do that for you when you want it done again.'

It was not very long before it wanted to be done again; and then Meg by daylight went through the contents of the box, choosing out those things which could best be spared, but leaving Robin's and baby's fine clothes to the last. She clung to these with a strong desire to save them, lest it should happen that her father came home too poor to redeem them. The packet of money, tied up and sealed, fell at last to the bottom of the almost empty box, and rolled noisily about whenever it was moved, but no thought of taking any of it entered into Meg's head. She was almost afraid of looking at it herself, lest the secret of it being there should get known in Angel Court; and whenever she mentioned it in her prayers, which she did every night, asking God to take care of it, she did not even whisper the words, much less speak them aloud, as she did her other requests, but she spoke inwardly only, for fear lest the very walls themselves should hear her. No one came near her attic, except Kitty, and she kept her promise faithfully. Since the four bearers had carried away her mother's coffin, and since the night Kitty came out of jail, the night of Robin's birthday, no stranger's foot had crossed the door-sill.

But November passed, and part of December, and Meg's stock of clothes, such as were of any value at the pawn-shop, was almost exhausted. At the end of the year the term for which her father had paid rent in advance would be over, and Mr Grigg might turn her and her children out into the streets. What was to be done? How was she to take care of Robin, and baby, and the money belonging to one of father's mates?

CHAPTER IX

Little Meg's Friends in Need

These were hard times for little Meg. The weather was not severely cold yet, or the children would have been bitterly starved up in their cold attic, where Meg was obliged to be very careful of the coal. All her mother's clothes were in pledge now, as well as her own and Robin's; and it seemed as if it would soon come to pawning their poor bed and their scanty furniture. Yet Meg kept up a brave spirit, and, as often as the day was fine enough, took her children out into the streets, loitering about the cook-shops, where the heat from the cellar kitchens lent a soothing warmth to their shivering bodies.

About the middle of December the first sharp frost set in, and Meg felt herself driven back from this last relief. She had taken the children out as usual, but she had no shoes to put on their feet, and nothing but their thin old rags to clothe them with. Robin's feet were red and blue with cold, like her own; but Meg could not see her own, and did not feel the cold as much for them as for Robin's. His face had lost a little of its roundness and freshness, and his black eyes some of their brightness since his birthday; and poor Meg's heart bled at the sight of him as he trudged along the icy pavement of the streets at her side. There was one cook-shop from which warm air and pleasant odours came up through an iron grating, and Meg hurried on to it to feel its grateful warmth; but the shutters of the shop were not taken down, and the cellar window was unclosed. Little Meg turned away sadly, and bent her bare and aching feet homewards again, hushing baby, who wailed a pitiful low wail in her ears. Robin, too, dragged himself painfully along, for he had struck his numbed foot against a piece of iron, and the wound was bleeding a little. They had turned down a short street which they had often passed through before, at the end of which was a small shop, displaying in its window a few loaves of bread, and some bottles containing different kinds of sweetmeats, such as they had indulged in sometimes in the palmy days when father was at home. The door was divided in the middle, and the lower half was closed, while the upper stood open, giving a full view of the shop within. Meg's old brown bonnet just rose above the top of the closed half, and her wistful face turned for a moment towards the tempting sight of a whole shelf full of loaves; but she was going on slowly, when a kindly voice hailed her from the dark interior.

'Hollo, little woman!' it shouted, 'I haven't set eyes on you this many a day. How's Robbie and baby.'

'They're here, sir, thank you,' answered Meg, in a more womanly way than ever, for she felt very low to-day. 'We're only doing middling, thank you, sir.'

'Why, father's ship's come in,' said her good-natured friend from the docks, coming forward and wiping his lips, as if he had just finished a good meal. 'What makes you be doing only middling?'

'Father didn't come home in the ship,' replied Meg, her voice faltering a little.

'Come in and tell us all about it,' he said. 'Hollo, Mrs Blossom! just step this way, if you please.'

There was a little kitchen at the back of the shop, from which came a very savoury smell of cooking, as the door opened, and a round, fat, rosy-cheeked woman, of about fifty years of age, looked out inquiringly. She came a step or two nearer the door, as Meg's friend beckoned to her with a clasp-knife he held in his hand.

'These little 'uns look cold and hungry, don't they, Mrs Blossom?' he said. 'You smell something as smells uncommon good, don't you?' he asked of Meg, who had sniffed a little, unconsciously.

'Yes, please, sir,' answered Meg.

'I've ate as much as ever I can eat for to-day,' said her friend, 'so you give 'em the rest, Mrs Blossom, and I'll be off. Only just tell me why father's not come home in his ship.'

'He was took bad on the other side of the world,' replied Meg, looking up tearfully into his good-tempered face, 'and they was forced to leave him behind in a hospital. That's why.'

'And what's mother doing?' he asked.

'Mother's dead,' she answered.

'Dead!' echoed her friend. 'And who's taking care of you young 'uns?'

'There's nobody to take care of us but God,' said Meg, simply and softly.

'Well, I never!' cried Mrs Blossom, seizing the baby out of Meg's, and clasping it in her own arms. 'I never heard anything like that.'

'Nor me,' said the man, catching up Robin, and bearing him off into the warm little kitchen, where a saucepan of hot tripe was simmering on the hob, and a round table, with two plates upon it, was drawn up close to the fire. He put Robin down on Mrs Blossom's seat, and lifted Meg into a large arm-chair he had just quitted.

'I guess you could eat a morsel of tripe,' he said, ladling it out in overflowing spoonfuls upon the plates. 'Mrs Blossom, some potatoes, if you please, and some bread; and do you feed the baby whilst the little woman gets her dinner. Now, I'm off. Mrs Blossom, you settle about 'em coming here again.'

He was off, as he said, in an instant. Meg sat in her large arm-chair, grasping a big knife and fork in her small hands, but she could not swallow a morsel at first for watching Robin and the baby, who was sucking in greedily spoonfuls of potatoes, soaked in the gravy. Mrs Blossom urged her to fall to, and she tried to obey; but her pale face quivered all over, and letting fall her knife and fork, she hid it in her trembling hands.

'If you please, ma'am, I'm only so glad,' said little Meg as soon as she could command her voice. 'Robbie and baby were so hungry, and I hadn't got anythink to give 'em.'

'I suppose you aint hungry yourself neither,' observed Mrs Blossom, a tear rolling down a little channel between her round cheeks and her nose.

'Oh, but ain't I!' said Meg, recovering herself still more. 'I've had nothink since last night, and then it were only a crust as Kitty give me.'

'Well, dear, fall to, and welcome,' answered Mrs Blossom. 'And who's Kitty?'

'It's a grown-up person as lives in the back attic,' answered Meg, after eating her first mouthful. 'She helps me all she can. She's took all my things to the pawn-shop for me, because she can get more money than me. She's as good as can be to us.'

'Are all your things gone to pawn?' inquired Mrs Blossom.

'I've got baby's cloak and hood left,' she replied mournfully. 'He wouldn't give more than a shilling for 'em, and I thought it wasn't worth while parting with 'em for that. I tried to keep Robbie's cap and pinafore, that were as good as new, but I were forced to let 'em go. And our shoes, ma'am,' added Meg, taking Robin's bare and bleeding foot into her hand: 'see what poor Robbie's done to himself.'

'Poor little dear!' said Mrs Blossom pityingly. 'I'll wash his poor little feet for him when he's finished his dinner. You get on with yours likewise, my love.'

Meg was silent for some minutes, busily feasting on the hot tripe, and basking in the agreeable warmth of the cosy room. It was a wonderfully bright little spot for that quarter of London, but the brightness was all inside. Outside, at about three feet from the window, rose a wall so high as to shut out every glimpse of the sky; but within everything was so clean and shining, even to the quarried floor, that it was difficult to believe in the mud and dirt of the streets without. Mrs Blossom herself looked fresh and comely, like a countrywoman; but there was a sad expression on her round face, plain enough to be seen when she was not talking.

'My dear,' she said when Meg laid down her knife and fork, and assured her earnestly that she could eat no more, 'what may you be thinking of doing?'

'I don't hardly know,' she answered. 'I expect father home every day. If I could only get enough for the children, and a crust or two for me, we could get along. But we can't do nothink more, I know.'

'You'll be forced to go into the house,' said Mrs Blossom.

'Oh, no, no, no!' cried little Meg, drawing Robin to her, and with a great effort lifting him on to her lap, where he almost eclipsed her. 'I couldn't ever do that. We'll get along somehow till father comes home.'

'Where is it you live?' inquired Mrs Blossom.

'Oh, it's not a nice place at all,' said Meg, who dreaded having any visitor. 'It's along Rosemary Lane, and down a street, and then down another smaller street, and up a court. That's where it is.'

Mrs Blossom sat meditating a few minutes, with the baby on her lap, stretching itself lazily and contentedly before the fire; while Meg, from behind Robin, watched her new friend's face anxiously.

'Well,' she said, 'you come here again to-morrow, and I'll ask Mr George what's to be done. That was Mr George as was here, and he's my lodger. He took you in, and maybe he'll agree to do something.'

'Thank you, ma'am,' said Meg gratefully. 'Please, have you any little children of your own?'

The tears ran faster now down Mrs Blossom's cheeks, and she was obliged to wipe them away before she could answer.

'I'd a little girl like you,' she said, 'ten years ago. Such a pretty little girl, so rosy, and bright, and merry, as all the folks round took notice of. She was like the apple of my eye, she was.'

'What was she called?' asked Meg, with an eager interest.

'Why, the neighbours called her Posy because her name was Blossom,' said Mrs Blossom, smiling amidst her tears. 'We lived out in the country, and I'd a little shop, and a garden, and kept fowls, and pigs, and eggs; fresh eggs, such as the like are never seen in this part o' London. Posy they called her, and a real posy she was.'

Mrs Blossom paused, and looked sadly down upon the happy baby, shaking her head as if she was sorely grieved at heart.

'And Posy died?' said Meg softly.

'No, no!' cried Mrs Blossom. 'It 'ud been a hundred times better if she'd died. She grew up bad. I hope you'll never live to grow up bad, little girl. And she ran away from home; and I lost her, her own mother that had nursed her when she was a little baby like this. I'd ha' been thankful to ha' seen her lying dead afore my eyes in her coffin.'

'That's bad,' said little Meg, in a tone of trouble and tender pity.

'It's nigh upon three years ago,' continued Mrs Blossom, looking down still upon the baby, as if she were telling her; 'and I gave up my shop to my son's wife, and come here, thinking maybe she'd step in some day or other to buy a loaf of bread or something, because I knew she'd come up to London. But she's never so much as passed by the window—leastways when I've been watching, and I'm always watching. I can't do my duty by Mr George for staring out o' the window.'

'Watching for Posy?' said little Meg.

'Ay, watching for Posy,' repeated Mrs Blossom, 'and she never goes by.'

'Have you asked God to let her go by?' asked Meg.

'Ay, my dear,' said Mrs Blossom. 'I ask Him every blessed day o' my life.'

'Then she's sure to come some day,' said Meg joyfully. 'There's no mistake about that, because Jesus says it in the Bible, and He knows all about God. You've asked Him, and He'll do it. It's like father coming. I don't know whether he'll come to-day or to-morrow, or when it'll be; but he will come.'

'God bless and love you!' cried Mrs Blossom, suddenly putting baby down in Meg's lap, and clasping all three of them in her arms. 'I'll believe it, I will. He's sent you to give me more heart. God love you all!'

It was some while before Mrs Blossom regained her composure; but when she did, and it was time for Meg and the children to go home before it was quite dark, she bound up Robin's foot in some rags, and gave Meg a loaf to carry home with her, bidding her be sure to come again the next day. Meg looked back to the shop many times before turning the corner of the street, and saw Mrs Blossom's round face, with its white cap border, still leaning over the door, looking after them, and nodding pleasantly each time she caught Meg's backward glance. At the corner they all three turned round, Meg holding up baby as high as her arms could reach, and after this last farewell they lost sight of their new friend.

CHAPTER X

Little Meg as Charwoman

Meg and her children did not fail to make their appearance the next morning at Mrs Blossom's shop, where she welcomed them heartily, and made them comfortable again by the kitchen fire. When they were well warmed, and had finished some bread, and some coffee which had been kept hot for them, Mrs Blossom put on a serious business air.

'Mr George and me have talked you over,' she said, 'and he's agreed to something. I can't do my duty by him as I should wish, you know why; and I want a little maid to help me.'

'Oh, if you please,' faltered little Meg, 'I couldn't leave our attic. I promised mother I wouldn't go away till father comes home. Don't be angry, please.'

'I'm not angry, child,' continued Mrs Blossom. 'I only want a little maid to come mornings, and go away nights, like a char-woman.'

'Mother used to go charing sometimes,' remarked Meg.

'I'm not a rich woman,' resumed Mrs Blossom, 'and Mr George has his old father to keep, as lives down in my own village, and I know him well; so we can't give great wages. I'd give you a half-quartern loaf a day, and Mr George threepence for the present, while it's winter. Would that suit your views?'

'What could I do with Robbie and baby?' asked Meg, with an air of perplexed thought.

'Couldn't you leave 'em with a neighbour?' suggested Mrs Blossom.

Meg pondered deeply for a while. Kitty had told her the night before that she had got some sailors' shirts to sew, and would stay at home to make them. She could trust Robin and the baby with Kitty, and instead of lighting a fire in her own attic she could give her the coals, and so save her fuel, as part payment for taking charge of the children. Yet Meg felt a little sad at the idea of leaving them for so long a time, and seeing so little of them each day, and she knew they would miss her sorely. But nothing else could be done, and she accepted Mrs Blossom's offer thankfully.

'You needn't be here afore nine o' the morning,' said Mrs Blossom; 'it's too early for Posy to be passing by; and you can go away again as soon as it's dark in the evening. You mustn't get any breakfast, you know, because that's in our bargain; and I'd never grudge you a meal's meat for the children either, bless 'em! They shall come and have a good tea with us sometimes, they shall—specially on Sundays, when Mr George is at home; and if you'd only got your clothes out o' pawn, we'd all go to church together. But we'll see, we'll see.'

Meg entered upon her new duties the next morning, after committing the children, with many lingering kisses and last good-byes, into Kitty's charge, who promised faithfully to be as kind to them as Meg herself. If it had not been for her anxiety with regard to them, she would have enjoyed nothing better than being Mrs Blossom's little maid. The good woman was so kindly and motherly that she won Meg's whole heart; and to see her sit by the shop window, knitting a very large long stocking for Mr George, but with her eyes scanning every woman's face that went by, made her feel full of an intense and childish interest. She began herself to watch for Posy, as her mother described her; and whenever the form of a grown-up girl darkened the doorway, she held her breath to listen if Mrs Blossom called her by that pet name. Mr George also was very good to Meg in his bluff way, and bought her a pair of nearly new shoes with his first week's wages, over and above the threepence a day which he paid her. With Mrs Blossom she held many a conversation about the lost girl, who had grown up wicked, and was therefore worse than dead; and before long Mr George observed that Meg had done her a world of good.

Christmas Day was a great treat to Meg; for though Mr George went down into the country to see his old father, Mrs Blossom invited her and the children to come to dinner, and to stay with her till it was the little ones' bedtime. When they sat round the fire in the afternoon she told them wonderful stories about the country—of its fields, and gardens, and lanes.

'I like gardens,' said Robin, 'but I don't like lanes.'

'Why don't you like lanes?' asked Mrs Blossom.

'I know lots of lanes,' he answered. 'There's Rosemary Lane, and it's not nice, nor none of 'em. They ain't nice like Temple Gardens.'

'Rosemary Lane!' repeated Mrs Blossom. 'Why, the lanes in the country are nothing like the lanes in London. They're beautiful roads, with tall trees growing all along 'em, and meeting one another overhead; and there are roses and honeysuckles all about the hedges, and birds singing, and the sun shining. Only you don't know anything about roses, and honeysuckles, and birds.'

'Are there any angels there?' asked Robin, fastening his glistening eyes upon her intently.

'Well, no,' said Mrs Blossom, 'not as I know of.'

'Is the devil in the country?' pursued Robin.

'Yes,' answered Mrs Blossom, 'I suppose he's there pretty much the same as here. Folks can be wicked anywhere, or else my Posy wouldn't have grown up bad.'

Robin asked no more questions, and Mrs Blossom was glad to talk of something else. It was a very happy day altogether, but it came too quickly to an end. Meg wrapped up her children well before turning out into the cold streets, and Mrs Blossom gave them a farewell kiss each, with two to Meg because she was such a comfort to her.

When they reached their own attic they heard Kitty call to them, and Meg opened her door. She was sitting without any fire, stitching away as for her life at a coarse striped shirt, lighted only by a small farthing candle; but she laid down her task for a minute, and raised her thin pale face, and her eyes half blinded with tears and hard work.

'Where have you been all day, little Meg?' she asked.

'Me and the children have been at Mrs Blossom's, answered Meg, 'because it's Christmas Day: and I wish you'd been there as well, Kitty. We'd such a good dinner and tea. She gave me a bit of cake to bring home, and you shall have some of it.'

'No, no,' said Kitty, 'it 'ud choke me.'

'Oh, it couldn't; it's as nice as nice can be,' said Meg. 'You must just have a taste of it.'

'Did you go talking about that Posy again?' asked Kitty, bending diligently over her work.

'We always talk about her,' answered Meg, 'every day. Mrs Blossom's watching for her to go by all day long, you know.'

'She'll never go by,' said Kitty shortly.

'Oh, she's certain sure to go by some day,' cried Meg. 'Mrs Blossom asks God to let her go by, every day of her life; and He's positive to do it.'

'If she's grown up so wicked,' argued Kitty, 'she didn't ought to go back to her mother, and her such a good woman. God won't send her back to her mother, you'll see.'

'But if God sent her back, her mother 'ud never think of her being wicked, she loves her so,' said little Meg. 'If Robbie were ever so naughty, I'd keep on loving him till he was good again.'

'Well, Posy'll never go home no more,' said Kitty; and hot tears fell fast upon her work.

'She will, she will,' cried Meg. 'I expect her every day, like father. Perhaps they'll both come home to-morrow. I wish you'd ask God to let Posy and father come home to-morrow.'

'I'm too bad to ask God for anything,' sobbed Kitty.

'Well, I don't know,' said Meg sorrowfully. 'You're not bad to me or the children. But I must go to bed now. Let us kiss you afore we go. Mrs Blossom kissed me twice, and said I was a comfort to her.'

Kitty threw down her work, and clasped Meg strongly in her arms, pressing down Meg's head upon her breast, and crying, 'Oh, my dear little Meg! My good little Meg!' Then she put them all three gently out of her room, and bade them good-night and God bless them, in a husky and tremulous voice.

CHAPTER XI

Little Meg's Baby

The new year came, but Meg's father had not arrived. Kitty was having a mad outburst, as if she had so long controlled herself that now it was necessary to break out into extra wickedness. She came home late every night, very drunk, and shouting loud snatches of songs, which wakened up the inmates of the lower stories, and drew upon her a storm of oaths. But she continued always good-natured and kind to Meg, and insisted upon having the daily charge of Robin and the baby, though Meg left them in her care with a very troubled and anxious spirit. Things were looking very dark to the poor little woman; but she kept up as brave a heart as she could, waiting from day to day for that long-deferred coming of her father, in which she believed so firmly.

It was a little later than usual one evening, for the days were creeping out since the new year, when Meg climbed wearily upstairs to Kitty's attic, in search of her children, but found that they were not there. Mr Grigg told her that he had seen Kitty take them out with her in the afternoon; and even while he was speaking, Meg saw her staggering and rolling into the court, with the baby fast asleep in her drunken arms. Meg took it from her without a word, and led Robin away upstairs. Robin's face was flushed, and his hand was very hot; but the baby lay in her arms heavily, without any movement or sign of life, except that the breath came through her parted lips, and her eyelids stirred a little. Meg locked the door of her attic, and laid her baby on the bed, while she lighted the fire and got their tea ready. Robin looked strange, but he chattered away without ceasing, while he watched her set the things in readiness. But the baby would not awake. It lay quite still on Meg's lap, and she poured a little warm tea into its mouth, but it did not swallow it, only slept there with heavy eyelids, and moving neither finger nor foot, in a strange, profound slumber. It was smaller and thinner than when mother died, thought Meg; and she lifted up the lifeless little hand to her lips, half hoping that its eyes would unclose a little more, and that sweet, loving smile, with which it always welcomed her return, would brighten its languid face. But baby was too soundly asleep to smile.

Little Meg sat up all night, with the baby lying on her lap, moaning a little now and then as its slumbers grew more broken, but never lifting up its eyelids to look into her face and know it. When the morning dawned it was still the same. Could the baby be ill? asked Meg of herself. It did not seem to be in any pain; yet she carried it to the door, and called softly for Kitty to come and look at it; but there was no reply, only from below came up harsh sounds of children screaming and angry women quarrelling.

Oaths and threats and shrieks were all the answer Meg's feeble cry received. She sat down again on her mother's low chair before the fire, and made the baby comfortable on her lap; while Robin stood at her knee, looking down pitifully at the tiny, haggard, sleeping face, which Meg's little hand could almost cover. What was she to do? There was no one in Angel Court whom she dare call to her help. Baby might even die, like the greater number of the babies born in that place, whose brief lives ended quickly, as if existence was too terrible a thing in the midst of such din and squalor. At the thought that perhaps baby was going to die, two or three tears of extreme anguish rolled down little Meg's cheeks, and fell upon baby's face; but she could not cry aloud, or weep many tears. She felt herself falling into a stupor of grief and despair, when Robin laid his hand upon her arm.

'Why don't you ask God to waken baby?' he asked.

'I don't know whether it 'ud be a good thing,' she answered. 'Mother said she'd ask Him over and over again to let her take baby along with her, and that 'ud be better than staying here. I wish we could all go to heaven; only I don't know whatever father 'ud do if he come home and found us all dead.'

'Maybe God'll take me and baby,' said Robbie thoughtfully, 'and leave you to watch for father.'

'I only wish baby had called me Meg once afore she went,' cried little Meg.

The baby stirred a little upon her knees, and stretched out its feeble limbs, opening its blue eyes wide and looking up into her face with its sweet smile of welcome. Then the eyelids closed again slowly, and the small features put on a look of heavenly calm and rest. Meg and Robin gazed at the change wonderingly without speaking; but when after a few minutes Meg laid her hand gently upon the smooth little forehead, the same chill struck to her heart as when she had touched her mother's dead face.

It did not seem possible to little Meg that baby could really be dead. She chafed its puny limbs, as she had seen her mother do, and walked up and down the room singing to it, now loudly, now softly; but no change came upon it, no warmth returned to its death-cold frame, no life to its calm face. She laid it down at length upon the bed, and crossed its thin wee arms upon its breast, and then stretching herself beside it, with her face hidden from the light, little Meg gave herself up to a passion of sorrow.

'If I'd only asked God, for Christ's sake,' she cried to herself, 'maybe He'd have let baby wake, though I don't know whether it's a good thing. But now she's gone to mother, and father'll come home, and he'll find nobody but me and Robbie, and the money safe. Oh! I wish I'd asked God.'

'Meg,' said Robin, after she had worn herself out with sobs and tears, and was lying silently beside baby, 'I'm very poorly. I think I'll go to live with the angels, where mother and baby are gone.'

Meg started up, and gazed anxiously at Robin. His bright eyes were dimmed, and his face was flushed and heavy; he was stretched on the floor near the fire, in a listless attitude, and did not care to move, when she knelt down beside him, and put her arm under his head. It ached, he said; and it felt burning hot to her touch. Meg's heart stood still for a moment, and then she dropped her tear-stained sorrowful face upon her hands.

'Pray God,' she cried, 'don't take Robbie away as well as baby. Maybe it wasn't a good thing for baby to stay, now mother's dead, though I've done everythink I could, and there's been nobody to take care of us but You. But, pray God, do let Robbie stay with me till father comes home; for Jesus Christ's sake. Amen.'

Meg rose from her knees, and lifted up Robin as gently as she could, soothing him, and talking fondly to him as she took off his clothes. When that was finished she laid him on the same bed where the baby was sleeping its last long sleep, with its tiny face still wearing an unspeakable calm; for Robin's little mattress had been sold some time ago. The day was just at an end, that sorrowful day, and a lingering light from the west entered through the attic window, and lit up the white, peaceful features with the flushed and drowsy face of Robin beside it. Meg felt as if her heart would surely break as she stooped over them, and kissed them both, her lips growing cold as they touched baby's smiling mouth. Then drawing her old shawl over her head, she locked the attic door securely behind her, and ran as fast as her feet could carry her to Mrs Blossom's house.

'Robbie's very ill,' gasped Meg, breathlessly, as she burst into the shop, the shutters of which were already put up, though it was still early in the night, 'and I want a doctor for him. Where shall I find a doctor?'

Mrs Blossom had her bonnet and cloak on, and looked very pale and flurried. When she answered Meg she kept her hand pressed against her heart.

'I'm just a-going to one,' she said, 'the best at this end o' London, Dr Christie, and you'd better come along with me. He knows me well. Meg, I've seen somebody go by to-day as was like Posy, only pale and thin; but when I ran out, she was gone like a shadow. I'm a-going to tell Dr Christie; he knows all about Posy and me.'

But Meg scarcely heard what Mrs Blossom said. All her thoughts and interest centred in Robin, and she felt impatient of the slow progress of her companion. They seemed to her to be going a long, long way, until they came to better streets and larger houses; and by-and-by they saw a carriage standing before a door, and a gentleman came out and got into it hurriedly.

'Why, bless me!' exclaimed Mrs Blossom, 'there's Dr Christie. Stop him, Meg, stop him!'

Meg needed no urging, but rushed blindly across the street. There was all at once a strange confusion about her, a trampling of horses' feet, and a rattling of wheels, with a sudden terror and pain in herself; and then she knew no more. All was as nothing to her—baby and Robin alone in the attic, and Mrs Blossom and Posy—all were gone out of her mind and memory. She had thrown herself before the horses' heads, and they had trampled her down under their feet.

When little Meg came to herself again it was broad daylight, and she was lying in a room so bright and cheerful that she could neither imagine where she was nor how she came there. There was a good fire crackling noisily in the low grate, with a brass guard before it, and over the chimney-piece was a pretty picture of angels flying upwards with a child in their arms. All round the walls there hung other pictures of birds and flowers, coloured gaily, and glittering in gilded frames. Another little bed like the one she lay in stood in the opposite corner, but there was nobody in it, and the place was very quiet. She lay quite still, with a dreamy thought that she was somehow in heaven, until she heard a pleasant voice speaking in the next room, the door of which was open, so that the words came readily to her ears.

'I only wish we knew where the poor little thing comes from,' said the voice.

'I'm vexed I don't,' answered Mrs Blossom. 'I've asked her more than once, and she's always said it's down a street off Rosemary Lane, and along another street, and up a court. But there's a girl called Kitty living in the back attic, as takes care of the children when Meg's away. She's sure to be taking care o' them now.'

In an instant memory came back to little Meg. She recollected bending over Robin and the baby to kiss them before she came away, and locking the door safely upon them. Oh! what had become of Robbie in the night? She raised herself up in bed, and uttered a very bitter cry, which brought to her quickly Mrs Blossom and a strange lady.

'I want Robbie,' she cried. 'I must get up and go to him directly. It's my Robbie that's ill, and baby's dead. I'm not ill, but Robbie's ill, if he isn't dead, like baby, afore now. Please to let me get up.'

'Tell me all about it,' said Mrs Blossom, sitting down on the bed and taking Meg into her arms. 'We're in Dr Christie's house, and he'll go and see Robbie in a minute, he says.'

'Baby died yesterday morning,' answered Meg, with tearless eyes, for her trouble was too great for tears; 'and then Robbie was took ill, and I put them both in bed, and kissed them, and locked the door, and came away for a doctor, and there's been nobody to take care of 'em all night, only God.'

Meg's eyes burned no longer, but filled with tears as she thought of God, and she laid her head upon Mrs Blossom's shoulder, and wept aloud.

'God has taken care of them,' said Mrs Christie, but she could say no more.

'Where is it you live, deary?' asked Mrs Blossom.

'It's at Angel Court,' answered Meg. 'But there mustn't nobody go without me. Please to let me get up. I'm not ill.'

'You're very much bruised and hurt, my poor child,' said Mrs Christie.

'I must go,' pleaded Meg urgently, 'I must get up, I promised mother I'd never let anybody go into our room, and they mustn't go without me. They're my children, please. If your little children were ill, you'd go to 'em wouldn't you? Let me get up this minute.'

It was impossible to withstand little Meg's earnestness. Mrs Blossom dressed her tenderly, though Meg could not quite keep back the groan which rose to her quivering lips when her bruised arm was moved. A cab was called, and then Mrs Blossom and Meg, with Dr Christie, got into it, and drove away quickly to Angel Court.

CHAPTER XII

The End of Little Meg's Trouble

It was early in the evening after Meg had gone in search of a doctor, that Kitty came home, more sober than she had been for several nights, and very much ashamed of her last outbreak. She sat down on the top of the stairs, listening for little Meg to read aloud, but she heard only the sobs and moanings of Robin, who called incessantly for Meg, without getting any answer. Kitty waited for some time, hearkening for her voice, but after a while she knocked gently at the door. There was no reply, but after knocking again and again she heard Robin call out in a frightened tone.

'What's that?' he cried.

'It's me, your own Kitty,' she said; 'where's little Meg?'

'I don't know,' said Robin, 'she's gone away, and there's nobody but me and baby; and baby's asleep, and so cold.'

'What are you crying for, Robbie?' asked Kitty.

'I'm crying for everything,' said Robin.

'Don't you be frightened, Robbie,' she said soothingly; 'Kitty'll stay outside the door, and sing pretty songs to you, till Meg comes home.'

She waited a long time, till the clocks struck twelve, and still Meg did not come. From time to time Kitty spoke some reassuring words to Robin, or sang him some little songs she remembered from her own childhood; but his cries grew more and more distressing, and at length Kitty resolved to break her promise, and unlock Meg's door once again to move the children into her own attic.

She lit a candle, and entered the dark room. The fire was gone out, and Robin sat up on the pillow, his face wet with tears and his black eyes large with terror. The baby, which lay beside him, seemed very still, with its wasted puny hands crossed upon its breast; so quiet and still that Kitty looked more closely, and held the light nearer to its slumbering face. What could ail it? What had brought that awful smile upon its tiny face? Kitty touched it fearfully with the tip of her finger; and then she stood dumb and motionless before the terrible little corpse.

She partly knew, and partly guessed, what had done this thing. She recollected, but vaguely enough, that one of her companions, who had grown weary of the little creature's pitiful cry, had promised to quiet it for her, and how speedily it had fallen off into a profound, unbroken slumber. And there it lay, in the same slumber perhaps. She touched it again; but no, the sleep it slept now was even deeper than that—a sleep so sound that its eyelids would never open again to this world's light, nor its sealed lips ever utter a word of this world's speech. Kitty could scarcely believe it; but she could not bear to stay in that mute, gentle, uncomplaining presence; and she lifted up Robin to carry him into her own room. Oh that God had but called her away when she was an innocent baby like that!

Robin's feverishness was almost gone; and now, wrapped in Kitty's gown and rocked to sleep on her lap, he lay contented and restful, while she sat thinking in the dark, for the candle soon burned itself out, until the solemn grey light of the morning dawned slowly in the east. She had made up her mind now what she would do. There was only one more sin lying before her. She had grown up bad, and broken her mother's heart, and now she had brought this great overwhelming sorrow upon poor little Meg. There was but one end to a sinful life like hers, and the sooner it came the better. She would wait till

Meg came home and give up Robin to her, for she would not hurry on to that last crime before Meg was there to take care of him. Then she saw herself stealing along the streets, down to an old pier she knew of, where boats had ceased to ply, and where no policeman would be near to hinder her, or any one about to rescue her; and then she would fling herself, worthless and wretched as she was, into the rapid river, which had borne so many worthless wretches like her upon its strong current into the land of darkness and death, of which she did not dare to think. That was what she would do, saying nothing to any one; and if she could ask anything of God, it would be that her mother might never find out what had become of her.

So Kitty sat with her dark thoughts long after Angel Court had awakened to its ordinary life, its groans, and curses, and sobs; until the sun looked in cheerily upon her and Robin, as it did upon Meg in Mrs Christie's nursery. She did not care to put him down, for he looked very pretty, and happy, and peaceful in his soft sleep, and whenever she moved he stirred a little, and pouted his lips as if to reproach her. Besides, it was the last time she would hold a child in her arms; and though they ached somewhat, they folded round him fondly. At last she heard a man's step upon the ladder mounting to the attics, and Meg's voice speaking faintly. Could it be that her father was come home at last? Oh! what would their eyes see when they opened that door? Kitty held her breath to listen for the first sound of anguish and amazement; but it was poor little Meg's voice which reached her before any other.

'Robbie! oh, Robbie!' she cried, in a tone of piercing terror, 'what has become of my little Robbie?'

'He's safe, he's here, Meg,' answered Kitty, starting to her feet, and rushing with him to Meg's attic.

It was no rough, weather-beaten seaman, who was just placing Meg on a chair, as if he had carried her upstairs; but some strange, well-clad gentleman, and behind him stood an elderly woman, who turned sharply round as she heard Kitty's voice.

'Posy!' cried Mrs Blossom.

No one but her own mother could have known again the bright, merry, rosy girl, whom the neighbours called Posy, in the thin, withered, pallid woman who stood motionless in the middle of the room. Even Meg forgot for a moment her fears for Robin. Dr Christie had only time to catch him from her failing arms, before she fell down senseless upon the floor at her mother's feet.

'Let me do everything for her,' exclaimed Mrs Blossom, pushing away Dr Christie; 'she's my Posy, I tell you. You wouldn't know her again, but I know her. I'll do everything for her; she's my girl, my little one; she's the apple of my eye.'

But it was a very long time before Mrs Blossom, with Dr Christie's help, could bring Posy to life again; and then they lifted her into her poor bed, and Dr Christie left her mother alone with her, and went back to Meg. Robin was ailing very little, he said: but the baby? Yes, the baby must have died even if little Meg had fetched him at once. Nothing could have saved it, and it had suffered no pain, he added tenderly.

'I think I must take you two away from this place,' said Dr Christie.

'Oh, no, no,' answered Meg earnestly; 'I must stay till father comes, and I expect him to-day or to-morrow. Please, sir, leave me and Robbie here till he comes.'

'Then you must have somebody to take care of you,' said Dr Christie.

'No, please, sir,' answered Meg, in a low and cautious voice, 'mother gave me a secret to keep that I can't tell to nobody, and I promised her I'd never let nobody come into my room till father comes home. I couldn't help you, and Mrs Blossom, and Kitty coming in this time; but nobody mustn't come in again.'

'My little girl,' said Dr Christie kindly, 'I dare say your mother never thought of her secret becoming a great trouble to you. Could you not tell it to me?'

'No,' replied Meg, 'it's a very great secret; and please, when baby's buried like mother, me and Robbie must go on living here alone till father comes.'

'Poor child!' said Dr Christie, rubbing his eyes, 'did you know baby was quite dead?'

'Yes,' she answered, 'but I didn't ask God to let baby live, because mother said she'd like to take her with her. But I did ask Him to make Robin well, and bring back Posy; and now there's nothing for Him to do but let father come home. I knew it was all true; it's in the Bible, and if I'm not one of God's own children, it says, "Them that ask Him." So I asked Him.'

Meg's voice sank, and her head dropped; for now that she was at home again, and Robin was found to be all right, her spirit failed her. Dr Christie went out upon the landing, and held a consultation with Mrs Blossom, in which they agreed that for the present, until Meg was well enough to take care of herself, she should be nursed in Kitty's attic, with her own door kept locked, and the key left in her possession. So Dr Christie carried Meg into the back attic, and laid her upon Kitty's mattress. Kitty was cowering down on the hearth, with her face buried on her knees, and did not look up once through all the noise of Meg's removal; though when her mother told her what they were doing she made a gesture of assent to it. Dr Christie went away; and Mrs Blossom, who wanted to buy many things which were sorely needed in the poor attic, put her arm fondly round Kitty's neck.

'Posy,' she said, 'you wouldn't think to go and leave little Meg alone if I went out to buy some things, and took Robin with me?'

'No, I'll stop,' said Kitty, but without lifting her head. When they were alone together, Meg raised herself as well as she could on the arm that was not hurt, and looked wistfully at Kitty's bowed-down head and crouching form.

'Are you really Posy?' she asked.

'I used to be Posy,' answered Kitty, in a mournful voice.

'Didn't I tell you God would let your mother find you?' said Meg; 'it's all come true, every bit of it.'

'But God hasn't let baby live,' muttered Kitty.

'I never asked Him for that,' she said falteringly; 'I didn't know as baby was near going to die, and maybe it's a better thing for her to go to mother and God. Angel Court ain't a nice place to live in, and she might have growed up bad. But if people do grow up bad,' added Meg, in a very tender tone, 'God can make 'em good again if they'd only ask Him.'

As little Meg spoke, and during the silence which followed, strange memories began to stir in the poor girl's heart, recalled there by some mysterious and Divine power. Words and scenes, forgotten since childhood, came back with wonderful freshness and force. She thought of a poor, guilty, outcast woman, reviled and despised by all save One, who had compassion even for her, forgave all her sins, stilled the clamour of her accusers, and said, 'Thy faith hath saved thee; go in peace.' She remembered the time when the records of His infinite love had been repeated by her innocent young lips and pondered in her maiden heart. Like some echo from the distant past she seemed to hear the words, 'By Thine agony and bloody sweat; by Thy cross and passion; by Thy precious death and burial, good Lord deliver us. O Lamb of God, that takest away the sins of the world, have mercy upon us.'

'Oh! Meg! Meg!' cried Kitty, almost crawling to the corner where she lay, and falling down beside her on the floor, with her poor pale face still hidden from sight, 'ask God for me to be made good again.'

Little Meg stretched out her unbruised arm, and laid her hand upon Kitty's bended head.

'You must ask Him for yourself,' she said, after thinking for a minute or two: 'I don't know as it 'ud do for me to ask God, if you didn't as well.'

'What shall I say, Meg?' asked Kitty.

'If I was you,' said Meg, 'and had grow'd up wicked, and run away from mother, I'd say, "Pray God, make me a good girl again, and let me be a comfort to mother till she dies; for Jesus Christ's sake. Amen."'

There was a dead silence in the back attic, except for the near noise and distant din which came from the court below, and the great labyrinth of streets around. Little Meg's eyes shone lovingly and pityingly upon Kitty, who looked up for an instant, and caught their light. Then she dropped her head down upon the mattress, and gave way to a storm of tears and sobs.

'O God,' she cried, 'do have mercy upon me, and make me good again, if it's possible. Help me to be a good girl to mother. God forgive me for Jesus Christ's sake!'

She sobbed out this prayer over and over again, until her voice fell into a low whisper which even Meg could not hear; and so she lay upon the floor beside the mattress until her mother came back. Mrs Blossom's face was pale, but radiant with gladness, and Posy looked at it for the first time fully. Then she gave a great cry of mingled joy and sorrow, and running to her threw her arms round her neck, and laid her face upon her shoulder.

'God'll hear me and have mercy upon me,' she cried. 'I'm going to be your Posy again, mother!'

CHAPTER XIII

Little Meg's Father

The baby was buried the next morning, after Meg had looked upon it for the last time lying very peacefully and smilingly in its little coffin, and had shed some tears that were full of sorrow yet had no bitterness upon its dead face. Mrs Blossom took Robin to follow it to the grave, leaving Kitty in charge of little Meg. The front attic door was locked, and the key was under Meg's pillow, not to be used again until she was well enough to turn it herself in the lock. The bag containing the small key of the box, with the unopened letter which had come for her mother, hung always round her neck, and her hand often clasped it tightly as she slept.

Meg was lying very still, with her face turned from the light, following in her thoughts the little coffin that was being carried in turns by Mrs Blossom and another woman whom she knew, through the noisy streets, when Kitty heard the tread of a man's foot coming up the ladder. It could be no one else but Dr Christie, she thought; but why then did he stop at the front attic door, and rattle the latch in trying to open it? Kitty looked out and saw a seafaring man, in worn and shabby sailor's clothing, as if he had just come off a long voyage. His face was brown and weather-beaten; and his eyes, black and bright, were set deep in his head, and looked as if they were used to take long, keen surveys over the glittering sea. He turned sharply round as Kitty opened her door.

'Young woman,' he said, 'do you know aught of my wife, Peggy Fleming, and her children, who used to live here? Peggy wrote me word she'd moved into the front attic.'

'It's father,' called little Meg from her mattress on the floor; 'I'm here, father! Robin and me's left; but mother's dead, and baby. Oh! father, father! You've come home at last!'

Meg's father brushed past Kitty into the room where Meg sat up in bed, her face quivering, and her poor bruised arms stretched out to welcome him. He sat down on the mattress and took her in his own strong arms, while for a minute or two Meg lay still in them, almost like one dead.

'Oh!' she said at last, with a sigh as if her heart had well-nigh broken, 'I've took care of Robin and the money, and they're safe. Only baby's dead. But don't you mind much, father; it wasn't a nice place for baby to grow up in.'

'Tell me all about it,' said Robert Fleming, looking at Kitty, but still holding his little daughter in his arms; and Kitty told him all she knew of her lonely life and troubles up in the solitary attic, which no one had been allowed to enter; and from time to time Meg's father groaned aloud, and kissed Meg's pale and wrinkled forehead fondly. But he asked how it was she never let any of the neighbours, Kitty herself, for instance, stay with her, and help her sometimes.

'I promised mother,' whispered Meg in his ear, 'never to let nobody come in, for fear they'd find out the box under the bed, and get into it somehow. We was afraid for the money, you know, but it's all safe for your mate, father; and here's the key, and a letter as came for mother after she was dead.'

'But this letter's from me to Peggy,' said her father, turning it over and over; 'leastways it was wrote by the chaplain at the hospital, to tell her what she must do. The money in the box was mine, Meg, no mate's; and I sent her word to take some of it for herself and the children.'

'Mother thought it belonged to a mate of yours,' said Meg, 'and we was the more afeared of it being stole.'

'It's my fault,' replied Robert Fleming. 'I told that to mother for fear she'd waste it if she knew it were mine. But if I'd only known—'

He could not finish his sentence, but stroked Meg's hair with his large hand, and she felt some hot tears fall from his eyes upon her forehead.

'Don't cry, father,' she said, lifting her small feeble hand to his face. 'God took care of us, and baby too, though she's dead. There's nothink now that He hasn't done. He's done everythink I asked Him.'

'Did you ask Him to make me a good father?' said Fleming.

'Why, you're always good to us, father,' answered Meg, in a tone of loving surprise. 'You never beat us much when you get drunk. But Robin and me always say, "Pray God, bless father." I don't quite know what bless means, but it's something good.'

'Ah!' said Fleming, with a deep sigh, 'He has blessed me. When I was ill He showed me what a poor sinner I was, and how Jesus Christ came into the world to save sinners, "of whom I am chief." Sure I can say that if anybody can. But it says in the Bible, "He loved me, and gave Himself for me." Yes, little Meg, He died to save me. I felt it. I believed it. I came to see that I'd nobody to fly to but Jesus if I wanted to be aught else but a poor, wicked, lost rascal, as got drunk, and was no better than a brute. And so I turned it over and over in my mind, lying abed; and now, please God, I'm a bit more like being a Christian than I was. I reckon that's what bless means, little Meg.'

As he spoke the door opened, and Mrs Blossom came in with Robin. It was twelve months since Robin had seen his father, and now he was shy, and hung back a little behind Mrs Blossom; but Meg called to him in a joyful voice.

'Come here, little Robbie,' she said; 'it's father, as we've watched for so long.—He's a little bit afeared at first, father, but you'll love him ever so when he knows you.'

It was not long before Robin knew his father sufficiently to accept of a seat on his knee, when Meg was put back into bed at Mrs Blossom's entreaties. Fleming nursed his boy in silence for some time, while now and then a tear glistened in his deep eyes as he thought over the history of little Meg's sorrows.

'I'm thinking,' said Mrs Blossom cheerfully, 'as this isn't the sort o' place for a widow man and his children to stop in. I'm just frightened to death o' going up and down the court. I suppose you're not thinking o' settling here, Mr Fleming?'

'No, no,' said Fleming, shaking his head: 'a decent man couldn't stop here, let alone a Christian.'

'Well, then, come home to us till you can turn yourself round,' continued Mrs Blossom heartily; 'me and Mr George have talked it over, and he says, "When little Meg's father do come, let 'em all come here: Posy, and the little 'uns, and all. You'll have Posy and the little 'uns in your room, and I'll have him in mine. We'll give him some sort o' a shakedown, and sailors don't use to lie soft." So if you've no objections to raise, it's settled; and if you have, please to raise 'em at once.'

Robert Fleming had no objections to raise, but he accepted the cordial invitation thankfully, for he was in haste to get out of the miserable life of Angel Court. He brought the hidden box into the back attic, and opened it before little Meg, taking out of it the packet of forty pounds, and a number of pawn-tickets, which he looked at very sorrowfully. After securing these he locked up the attic again, and carrying Meg in his arms, he led the way down the stairs, and through the court, followed closely by Mrs Blossom, Posy, and Robin. The sound of brawling and quarrelling was loud as usual, and the children crawling about the pavement were dirty and squalid as ever; they gathered about Meg and her father, forming themselves into a dirty and ragged procession to accompany them down to the street. Little Meg looked up to the high window of the attic, where she had watched so often and so long for her father's coming; and then she looked round, with eyes full of pity, upon the wretched group about her; and closing her eyelids, her lips moving a little, but without any words which even her father could hear, she said in her heart, 'Pray God, bless everybody, and make them good.'

CHAPTER XIV

Little Meg's Farewell

About a month after Robert Fleming's return Dr Christie paid a visit to Mrs Blossom's little house. He had been there before, but this was a special visit; and it was evident some important plan had to be decided upon. Dr Christie came to hear what Mrs Blossom had to say about it.

'Well, sir,' said Mrs Blossom, 'a woman of my years, as always lived in one village all her life till I came to London, it do seem a great move to go across the sea. But as you all think as it 'ud be a good thing for Posy, and as Mr Fleming do wish little Meg and Robin to go along with us, which are like my own children, and as he's to be in the same ship, I'm not the woman to say No. I'm a good hand at washing and ironing, and sewing, and keeping a little shop, or anything else as turns up; and there's ten years' good work in me yet; by which time little Meg'll be a stout, grown-up young woman; to say nothing of Posy, who's old enough to get her own living now. I can't say as I like the sea, quite the contrairy; but I can put up with it; and Mr Fleming'll be there to see as the ship goes all right, and doesn't lose hisself. So I'll be ready by the time the ship's ready.'

They were all ready in time as Mrs Blossom had promised, for there were not many preparations to be made. Little Meg's red frock was taken out of pawn, with all the other things, and Mrs Blossom went down to her native village to visit it for the last time; but Posy shrank from being seen there by the neighbours again. She, and Meg, and Robin went once more for a farewell look at Temple Gardens. It was the first time she had been in the streets since she had gone back to her mother, and she seemed ashamed and alarmed at every eye that met hers. When they stood looking at the river, with its swift, cruel current, Posy shivered and trembled until she was obliged to turn away and sit down on a bench. She was glad, she said, to get home again, and she would go out no more till the day came when Mr George drove them all down to the docks, with the few boxes which contained their worldly goods.

Dr Christie and his wife were down at the ship to see them off, and they kissed Meg tenderly as they bade her farewell. When the last minute was nearly come, Mr George took little Meg's small hand in his large one, and laid the other upon her head.

'Little woman, tell us that verse again,' he said, 'that verse as you've always gone and believed in, and acted on.'

'That as mother and me heard preached from the streets?' asked Meg.

Mr George nodded silently.

'It's quite true,' said little Meg, in a tone of perfect confidence, 'because it's in the Bible, and Jesus said it. Besides, God did everythink I asked Him. "If ye then, being evil, know how to give good gifts unto your children: how much more shall your Father which is in heaven give good things to them that ask Him?"'

SARAH SMITH (writing as Hesba Stretton) – A CONCISE BIBLIOGRAPHY

Short Stories & Periodicals
The Lucky Leg (19th March 1859)
The Ghost in the Clock Room (Christmas, 1859)
The Postmaster's Daughter (All the Year Round, 5th November 1859)
A Provincial Post Office (All the Year Round, 28 February 1863)
Jessica's First Prayer (Sunday at Home, July 1866)
The Travelling Post-Office (All the Year Round, Mugby Junction, December 1866)
Jessica's Mother (1867)

Books
Fern's Hollow (1864)
Enoch Roden's Training (1865)
The Children of Cloverley (1865)
Jessica's First Prayer (Sunday at Home, July 1866)
The Fishers of Derby Haven (1866)
Jessica's Mother (Periodical 1867, book 1904)
Pilgrim Street (1867)
Little Meg's Children (1868)
Alone in London (1869)
Nellie's Dark Days (1870)
The Doctor's Dilemma (1872)
The King's Servants (1873)
Lost Gip (1873
Cassy (1874)
Brought Home (1875)
In Prison and Out (1878)
Two Secrets (1882)
The Lord's Purse-Bearers (1883)
Sam Franklin's Savings Bank (1888)
Little Meg's Children (1905)
The Christmas Child (1909 in US)

Other Works

Brought Home
Cobwebs And Cables